His to Protect

Also from Carly Phillips

Rosewood Bay
Fearless
Breathe
Freed (coming late 2018)

Bodyguard Bad Boys
Rock Me
Tempt Me
His to Protect

Dare to Love Series
Dare to Love
Dare to Desire
Dare to Touch
Dare to Hold
Dare to Rock
Dare to Take

Dare NY Series (NY Dare Cousins)
Dare to Surrender
Dare to Submit
Dare to Seduce

Billionaire Bad Boys
Going Down Easy
Going Down Hard
Going Down Fast
Going In Deep

Hot Zone Series
Hot Stuff
Hot Number
Hot Item
Hot Property

Lucky Series
Lucky Charm
Lucky Streak
Lucky Break

His to Protect
By Carly Phillips

A Bodyguard Bad Boys/Masters and Mercenaries Novella

Introduction by Lexi Blake

EVIL EYE
CONCEPTS

His to Protect
A Bodyguard Bad Boys/Masters and Mercenaries Novella
Copyright 2018 Carly Phillips
ISBN: 978-1-945920-80-6

Published by Evil Eye Concepts, Incorporated

Sign up for the 1001 Dark Nights Newsletter
and be entered to win a Tiffany Lock necklace.

There's a contest every quarter!

Go to www.1001DarkNights.com to subscribe.

As a bonus, all subscribers will receive a free copy of
Discovery Bundle Three
Featuring stories by
Sidney Bristol, Darcy Burke, T. Gephart
Stacey Kennedy, Adriana Locke
JB Salsbury, and Erika Wilde

An Introduction to the Lexi Blake Crossover Collection

Who doesn't love a crossover? I know that for me there's always been something magical about two fictional words blending and meeting in a totally unexpected way. For years the only medium that has truly done it well and often is comic books. Superman vs. Batman in a fight to the finish. Marvel's Infinite Universe. There's something about two crazy worlds coming together that almost makes them feel more real. Like there's this brilliant universe filled with fictional characters and they can meet and talk, and sometimes they can fall in love.

I'm a geek. I go a little crazy when Thor meets up with Iron Man or The Flash and Arrow team up.

So why wouldn't we do it in Romanceland?

There are ways out there. A writer can write in another author's world, giving you her take on it. There's some brilliant fanfiction out there, but I wanted something different. I wanted to take my time and gradually introduce these characters from other worlds, bring you in slowly so you don't even realize what I'm doing. So you think this is McKay-Taggart, nothing odd here. Except there is…

Over the course of my last three books—Love Another Day, At Your Service, and Nobody Does It Better—I introduced you to five new characters and five new and brilliant worlds. If I've done my job, you'll know and love these characters—sisters from another mister, brothers from another mother.

So grab a glass of wine and welcome to the Lexi Blake Crossover Collection.

Love,

Lexi

Available now!

Close Cover by Lexi Blake
Her Guardian Angel by Larissa Ione
Justify Me by J. Kenner
Say You Won't Let Go by Corinne Michaels
His to Protect by Carly Phillips
Rescuing Sadie by Susan Stoker

Acknowledgments from the Author

To Liz Berry and MJ Rose and for making me part of the 1,001 Dark Nights family. Dreams really do come true. And to Lexi Blake for trusting me to write in your awesome and amazing world. I hope I did you justice.

Chapter One

Talia Shaw mentally ran through her to-do list, pleased with the outcome. Laundry folded and waiting to be put away. Dishwasher unloaded. All other household tasks complete with the afternoon to spare. She rarely took more than one day off a week from her job at Newton Laboratories, so chores tended to pile up.

Not that she had anything else to do. Work came first and it usually left little time for anything... or anyone else. She wasn't complaining. She happily lived and breathed her research.

She carried the full laundry basket into the bedroom, placing it on the bed just as her cell phone rang. Her assistant's name flashed on the screen, and she answered his call. "Hi, Chris."

Christopher Eldridge was the best assistant Talia had ever had. He worked the same long hours she did without complaint and was as dedicated to their current research as she was. Although her reasons were more personal.

"Chris?" she said again when he remained silent, only the sound of breathing on the other end.

"I'm at the lab and something's wrong," he said in a hushed whisper that wasn't at all like his normal moderate tone.

She narrowed her gaze. "What is it? What's going on?"

"Someone else is here and everything is—" Dead silence followed.

"Chris?" she asked again, but the call had obviously been cut off.

That was odd, she thought, nerves prickling along her skin. It wasn't unusual for her or Chris to go into work on a Sunday, but his low, raspy voice and the panicked tone, along with the insistence that something was wrong, weren't normal at all.

She wished she wasn't so paranoid, but she came by it naturally. Her mentor, Dr. Jonah Goodwin, was suspicious to the extreme, and he'd hammered into her the need to take precautions with every experiment and piece of work she was involved in. Especially now that she'd had success at last. It was that sense of caution and unease that had her hitting redial and calling Chris back.

Twice.

But voice mail picked up immediately each time.

She hung up and tapped the phone on the edge of the rubber basket, more than a little concerned. Was something wrong with their work? Could it be a problem with the last of the experiments they'd worked on before finalizing the formula? Possible, but he'd also said someone was *there*... Nothing made sense.

She bit down on her lower lip and decided to head over to the office and see what was going on for herself. Leaving her laundry on the bed, she grabbed her bag off the counter, picked up her keys and entry card, and climbed into her car.

She lived in an apartment close to the lab in the Arts District in downtown Dallas, and on a Sunday, she made it to the building, also downtown, in no time. The parking lot was nearly deserted, which she expected on the last day of the weekend. She saw Chris's Prius in his usual spot, but there was no sign of her assistant.

She pulled her car to an empty location near the door and rushed inside, expecting to find the security guard at his usual post, but his seat was empty. Damnit. She'd wanted him to accompany her to the lab, in case something really was wrong, as Chris had said.

She glanced around, but other than the tall potted plants lining the glass entryway, she was alone. Which could be explained by a possible bathroom break for the guard...if she ignored the tingling inside her that had begun with Chris's panicked, dropped call.

She had to see for herself. She swiped the card that let her past the metal barriers and headed into the elevators that took her to the fourth floor, where her lab was located. The doors opened to a quiet, empty floor. This was never a busy hallway during the week, so the silence didn't alarm her on the weekend.

She rounded the corner and reached her workshop. She glanced through the window and was struck dumb by the sight. Her computers on the countertops were gone. Experiment tables with microscopes and other equipment for her research, missing. Stark white walls and clean countertops gleamed through the glass, mocking her.

Her heart began to pound hard in her chest, and she debated what to do. Chris was nowhere to be found, and suddenly going inside the lab didn't seem smart, so she backed away from the door, just as the elevator around the corner dinged.

A man's voice sounded from around the corner. "I know she's here. Maybe I can trap her in the lab."

Shit. She had to get out of here. She started down the hall, in the opposite direction from the elevators, checking over her shoulder as she made her way to the stairwell. She pushed open the door just as the man's voice sounded again.

"No, I don't see her yet."

She stepped into the protection of the hall by the stairs and peeked out, but she didn't recognize the man in the dark suit. Fear rushed through her and perspiration dampened her skin beneath her shirt.

Talia ducked out of sight and listened because she needed some kind of information to know what the hell was going on. What she was dealing with.

"I still don't see her," he said from his position at the lab. "But she's in the building. Send backup."

Talia didn't wait another second. She eased the door closed without letting it make a sound, then ran down the stairs, treading lightly, grateful she had her ballet slipper shoes on to muffle the noise.

She needed to get the hell out of here. This staircase led to an exit on the side of the building near the parking lot. If the guy looking for her was the only one here now, she could run to her car and be gone before anyone else showed up. Opening the door would set off the alarms, but again…she had a chance of escape.

She had to take it.

Talia dug for her keys and held them in one hand. Then she drew in a deep breath and pushed open the door. Security alarms began blaring, but she ignored them, bolting for her car, not breaking stride as she fled across the green lawn and then onto the black asphalt.

She didn't look back the way she came or toward the front of the building, and she didn't hit the open button on her key fob until she was right next to the car door.

Climbing in, she locked the doors, started her small BMW, put the car in drive, and tore out of the parking lot, her pulse racing, sweat pouring down her neck, and panic rushing through her veins.

She forced herself to calm down and think for a minute. If everything was gone, someone had stolen her research. But they'd only get the final piece of the formula that comprised the treatment for a heart defect that would result in early death if not treated. She knew firsthand.

Absently, she rubbed the heart pendant she never took off, a gift from her mom, who had suffered with the congenital defect and died when Talia was only fourteen. She'd lost her dad to a heart attack when she was nineteen and away at college. To say treating heart ailments was her life's passion would be an understatement.

Talia's mentor had begun the work on the treatment, but ultimately he had retreated to his hermit life, and she had taken it over. But she'd listened to him and learned from his experience. She never kept all the pieces in one place. Just in case.

She and Chris had had a major breakthrough last week, and she'd informed her boss. Now everything in her lab was gone. She blew out a breath. Whoever had emptied her work space would soon find out they didn't have the whole formula... Or they already knew and wanted the rest of her research. The pieces she'd hidden.

She needed to figure out what to do. She'd spent many years working on the treatment for this congenital defect and had believed that Newton Laboratories, who subsidized her research, would bring it to market with a reputable pharmaceutical company. One that would do right by the people suffering.

Keeping one eye on the road and another on her rearview mirror, she drove, no destination in mind. She couldn't go home... If people were looking for her or the pieces of her work, they'd go there first. Not that they'd find anything, but she needed help.

She reached out one hand and dug through her purse for the familiar feel of her phone. A quick look down and she pulled up her favorites and hit the first person listed, her brother, Tate.

Tate and Talia. Her mother had loved the alliteration, bless her soul.

Talia hit send, fully aware it was twelve hours ahead in China, where he was visiting a client. Tate worked for Alpha Securities, a firm in New York, and he'd know exactly what she should do now.

He answered on the third ring. "Talia, what's wrong?" he

immediately asked, knowing she wouldn't wake him unless it was an emergency.

She swallowed hard, glancing again in the rearview mirror as she drove. "I was at my lab and someone's after me. I'm driving aimlessly and I—"

"Listen to me carefully," he said, and she could picture him sitting up in bed, hair sticking out, and barking orders.

His commanding voice soothed her frazzled nerves, as did the fact that he didn't ask for unnecessary details. He knew her job came with risks and certain dangers due to the high monetary stakes involved in drug development.

"Ditch the phone as soon as you hang up with me. Hop on 75 to Mockingbird and drive straight to Love Field," he said of the nearest airport. "Leave the car in long-term parking and take a cab to Shane Landon's house in Richardson."

The name conjured up all sorts of memories, some of them good, the last one between them utterly humiliating. She hadn't seen Shane since high school, but he and Tate were still friends. Since leaving the LAPD, Shane was a bodyguard. In fact, he sometimes freelanced for the firm where Tate worked in New York when they needed a hand.

Her brother had mentioned that much in her presence, and silly her, she'd catalogued any information on the sexy guy she'd stupidly pushed away in a teenage panic.

"Tali, are you listening?"

"Of course. Ditch the phone and leave the car in long-term parking."

"Take a cab to Shane's." He rattled off the address, knowing with her memory she'd caught it the first time. "And do not use a credit card. Cash only. Call me as soon as you get there so I know you're safe. Once Shane has details, he and I will make a plan."

"Got it," she said.

"I mean it. I'll worry, so make sure you call me."

"I know," she murmured, grateful for her older sibling's caring. Since losing both parents, they were all the family each had left and were extremely close, even with him living in Manhattan.

"I'll let Shane know you're on your way. Now go concentrate and watch for a tail."

"Believe me, I am." Not that she knew how to easily lose one if she discovered someone was following her. "Love you," she whispered.

"Back at you." He disconnected the call.

Talia glanced around her on the highway and realized there was nobody behind her. She pulled into the right lane, slowed a bit, opened the window, and with an apology to her life's information on that cell phone, tossed the piece of metal onto the side of the road.

A little while later, she'd left the car in a dark corner of long-term parking, walked quickly to the nearest taxi stand in the airport, and given the driver Shane Landon's address.

She ought to be nervous about seeing him again, but she couldn't concentrate on anything but the stranger who'd wanted to trap her in her lab—and wondered what he'd have done with her if he had.

She shivered in the back of the cab, touching the locket on her neck for comfort.

"Want me to turn on the radio?" the driver offered.

"No. Thank you." She just wanted to get to her destination so she could have the time to think and sort out the situation in her mind.

Finally, he pulled in front of a gorgeous home that was obviously new construction. She paid the driver the money she'd pulled out of her wallet—all the cash she'd had on her, and she was grateful she hadn't had to ask the man to wait so she could get money from Shane.

She stepped out of the cab, shut the door, and the taxi sped off, leaving her feeling open and exposed. She rushed to the front door, looking over her shoulder constantly, and rang the bell, followed by some banging with her hand.

A car door slammed in the distance, and she jumped a good ten feet, immediately banging her knuckles on the door again.

Obviously, Shane wasn't home, but just as clearly, she couldn't stand out here, causing a scene. Nor did she want to be out in the open. She didn't think anyone had followed her from the lab. They'd have shown themselves by now if they had, right? But still, she didn't want to take any chances.

She'd seen a gate around the side of the house when the cab had pulled up, so maybe she could hide in his backyard until he returned. She glanced around. Still no sign of cars or neighbors.

She followed the walkway toward the driveway, then headed to the gate around back. Tall wooden fencing blocked anyone from seeing in—or out—which afforded her the protection she needed, as long as the lock was open.

She reached for the latch…and bingo. She expelled a long sigh of relief as she pushed the heavy slats open and stepped inside, shutting the gate and clicking it closed behind her.

Alone in the big backyard, with a large in-ground pool in front of her, she felt her shoulders sag at the respite from the panic that had been accompanying her for the last hour. She wasn't out of danger, but at least she was marginally safe.

She exhaled hard and started for the patio chairs, planning to sit and catch her breath, when a deep thrum of music coming from the other side of the lawn caught her attention. The tunes played from speakers attached to the house.

She followed the sound to an outdoor shower stall. The swinging door was open wide, and Shane Landon stood inside, water sluicing down his tanned, muscular, completely naked body. His face was turned up toward the shower head, eyes closed, as he soaped up that glorious skin with his hands.

For a brief moment, the fear she'd been running from evaporated, and all she could concentrate on was him. His dark hair, wet from the shower, his biceps bulging as he rinsed off, the tattoos on his chest, and as her gaze traveled lower to his impressive package, her own body came to life. Her nipples puckered into tight points, arousal pulsing through her veins. She stared unabashedly until—

"What the fuck?" He slammed the shower off and stormed toward her, dripping wet, no towel in sight.

Obviously her brother hadn't been able to reach him. He'd been indisposed… And the events of the morning came flooding back. Chris's frightened call, finding her lab empty, her work gone, hiding from a man who'd wanted to trap her. It was like a thriller movie, but she was the one on the run, and this was her life.

The adrenaline that had guided her this far left her in a rush. "Shane," she said, her voice shaking.

"Talia?" He stared at her in disbelief.

"I need you." She took one step and her knees buckled.

He stepped forward and caught her before she hit the ground, his big, hard, naked body protecting hers with strength and heat.

Chapter Two

Shane grabbed Talia before her knees gave out and picked her up, carrying her to the reclining chairs where she could sit…and he could wrap himself in a towel. His dick was already reacting to having her in his arms, a warm, soft woman who smelled damned good.

She wasn't passed out cold, she'd just collapsed due to falling adrenaline, something he'd seen many times before on the force and in his work with security firms.

But why the fuck was she here now?

He set her on the reclining chair, and she pushed herself up against the back, breathing in and out slowly.

The familiar ring of his phone caught his attention. He glanced at the table where his cell sat… and saw her brother was calling.

Shane picked up quickly. "Hey, man."

"Where the hell have you been? I have an emergency."

"I was in the shower. But if you're calling about Talia," he said, glancing over to catch her staring at him, wide-eyed behind her black-framed glasses, "package arrived safely." He couldn't stop himself from winking at her.

And her cheeks flushed a pretty pink.

"She was supposed to let me know she was safe," Tate grumbled. "She's in trouble. She called from her lab and said someone was after her."

Shane narrowed his gaze, not liking the sound of that at all. "I'll get to the bottom of it," he promised, knowing his friend was in China and would be worried sick about his sister.

"Keep in touch," Tate demanded.

"Will do." Shane disconnected the call and looked at Talia.

A woman he hadn't seen since high school because, although he was good friends with her brother, he and Talia ran in different circles.

They always had.

A year younger, the little brainiac who'd tutored him in chemistry his senior year had saved his ass and enabled him to graduate. Too bad he'd been stupid enough to kiss her as a thank you, then shove his tongue down her throat and his hand up her shirt like she was a horny cheerleader and he was the football captain copping a feel. Which he had been.

But she wasn't that kind of girl. She'd deserved better. No wonder she'd pushed him away and slammed the door in his face, avoiding him afterward. Then life had taken them their separate ways.

But now she needed him and he found irony in that.

He had wrapped the towel around his waist and tucked the corner in to keep it in place. Folding his arms across his chest, he pinned her with his most serious gaze. "Tate says you're in trouble. And I can't help you unless I know the extent of it. So let's hear it," he said, getting down to what he did best.

Business.

Because if he kept staring at her porcelain skin, big brown doe eyes, and silky, chocolate-colored hair falling haphazardly and adorably out of a bun on the back of her head, his cock wouldn't go down and this situation would remain embarrassing. Apparently she still made him lose control just as she'd done years ago.

She pulled her jean-clad knees up to her chin, doing her best to keep her gaze on his chest and above, but she kept glancing down at the towel. And his dick liked the attention and stood in awareness.

Shit.

"Situation?" he barked at her, in a tone his ex-wife would have shrunk back from. No matter that he'd never take his frustration out on her. She wasn't the strong, silent type a cop had needed for a wife.

Talia didn't flinch. "I'm working on a treatment for a congenital heart defect. I found the answers, and today when I showed up at my lab, everything was gone. Wiped clean. And a big, burly guy was talking into his cell phone about trapping me in the lab and asking for backup before I left the building."

Shane's senses went on alert. Big pharma meant big money. Those people didn't play around. "If whoever is after you now has all your work and research, why do they need you?" he asked.

She bit down on her full bottom lip. "It's a long story."

He couldn't tear his stare from that puffy pink flesh. He wanted to draw it into his mouth for a taste. He frowned at the direction of his thoughts.

If he was going to help her, he needed to focus. "Were you followed here?" he asked.

"I don't think so." She shook her head, fingering a locket around her neck nervously.

"Not good enough. Come on. I'll get you something cold to drink and I'll get dressed." He extended a hand, and she grasped it so he could pull her to her feet.

He hadn't anticipated the jolt of awareness on contact, and he cleared his throat. "From there we'll go to my office and work out a game plan."

He started for the kitchen, knowing he had to call his boss and get some people in on the weekend to help out. Ian Taggart, head of McKay-Taggart Security Services, was a solid guy…who wouldn't appreciate being called away from his wife and kids on a weekend off. That said, as soon as he heard the story and Talia's connection to a man who was the closest thing Shane had to a brother, he'd drop everything and offer up MT services to help.

After he busted Shane's balls—because one look at Shane and Talia and the bastard would figure out there'd been something between them. Years ago or not, Ian would give him shit. Taggart was that good at reading people. Shane wondered if he had time to stop and pick up a lemon-filled dessert from Ian's brother Sean at his restaurant, Top. Anything lemon would take the edge off Ian's bite.

He glanced over his shoulder at Talia. No, no time to stop. Getting her safely to MT, where they could assess and work out a plan of action, was his main priority at the moment.

"Before we go to your office, I have to stop at my apartment," she said from behind him.

Shane opted to get them inside and lock the door behind them before he turned and scowled at her request. "Isn't that the first place someone would go? If they're looking for you?"

She nodded. "But you know that long story I mentioned? It

involves the research results and the way to reconstruct the treatment. And it's in pieces. Whoever stole my lab equipment only got the last part that my assistant and I just finished. The second part is hidden in a safe at my house."

He was afraid to ask where the first part was. Shane scrubbed a hand down his face. "Then I'll take you to McKay-Taggart, where you'll be safe, and I'll go pick up the work product."

"You can't do that!"

He shook his head, not planning on giving in on this. Her safety came first. "Now isn't the time to get stubborn. I protect you. That's my job."

"It's not being stubborn! My safe opens with my fingerprint." She met his gaze defiantly, hands on her sweet hips. "You need me with you. Or at least you need my finger and I'm pretty attached to it. In more ways than one."

He grinned, caught off guard that she could joke when she was also so afraid. He had to respect that about her. He didn't like it but she had a point.

"Fine. We go to your house first but you do everything—and I mean everything—I say. Agreed?"

"Agreed. Now can you do me a favor?" she asked.

He nodded. "Want that cold drink?"

She shook her head. "I want you to put some clothes on." Her cheeks burned as she spoke the words. But her point was clear.

She was as affected by him as he was by her. And they hadn't even had a chance to get reacquainted yet.

* * * *

Shane Landon had a great ass. With Talia's smarts and all the sudden insanity in her life, *that* was the main topic going through her mind. But as he walked away from her, towel low on his hips, his sexy ass was the best thing she could think about.

It was better than recalling how she'd collapsed against his naked body. Not that she didn't appreciate the feeling, and he'd smelled incredibly good, but it was another humiliating experience to add to the other mortifying incident with Shane. And while he was upstairs getting dressed, she had nothing but time to recall the first moment in excruciating detail.

She'd spent spring of her junior, his senior year in high school tutoring the hot jock in chemistry so he could graduate on time. The guy she had an insane crush on, and also her brother's best friend, was always surrounded by the prettiest, most popular girls in school. There was no way he'd be interested in a science geek like her. Even if he did tease her during their sessions, when his blue eyes would light up with laughter at her usually too complicated explanations before she *dumbed things down for him*, his words, not hers. She'd never thought he was dumb.

He would call her his little brainiac, or smarty-pants, and though if anyone else had said it, she'd think they were making fun of her, he always did it with a warm twinkle in his gaze and a little lift of his lips that she liked to think was just for her. Hey, a girl could dream, and she knew that's all she'd ever do about Shane Landon. Especially since she was always uncomfortable and inevitably did something awkward around him.

Yes, there was something about Shane that brought out the awkward girl inside her, and clearly that hadn't changed.

"I'm ready," he said, striding back into the kitchen, where he'd left her, this time fully dressed. He wore a dark pair of jeans and a light black jacket, which no doubt covered his weapon.

"Great." She swallowed hard, as things had just gotten *real*. Nothing said reality like a man with a gun. He shut off the music outside and the lights indoors.

She followed him to the garage, where he set the alarm to the house and held open the car door for her to climb inside his navy and khaki-colored Jeep Wrangler.

"What's your address?" he asked, and she rattled off the condo information.

He took off in his hot car. Her nerves had returned. If she wasn't so afraid, she'd enjoy the ride, but she couldn't stop wondering just what she was up against and why.

When she finally paid attention to her surroundings, she realized he was driving them in circles and taking off-the-beaten-path roads.

"Why—"

"Just in case you had a tail," he said, reading her mind before she could ask the question in full. "Now here's how it's going to go. We get to your place, I go first. You stay behind me. You pack up some clothes and necessities first. Five minutes and we're out of there. Put everything in a brown paper bag or bland shopping bag and we'll check it over at the office. Then we go to the safe at your apartment. We'll grab your work and get the hell out," he said, all sexy efficiency, his aviators covering his eyes as he glanced her way.

"Yes, boss." She saluted him because she was actually calmed by his list of commands.

He frowned at her, and she shook her head, knowing he'd thought she was being glib. "I'm serious. I'm not looking to get myself killed. I'll listen."

His shoulders eased down at her admission. "Where's the safe?" he asked her.

She couldn't help the self-satisfied smile that took hold. "Beneath the shower. It's waterproof." She was rather proud of her hiding place.

"Nice," he acknowledged and she grinned.

"Where are we going that I need clothes?" she asked.

"We'll figure that out at McKay-Taggart, but obviously you can't stay here," he said as he pulled into the parking lot of her co-op. "Ready?" he asked.

She blew out a shallow breath. "As I'll ever be. Let's do it."

He came around to her side and she followed him out of the car and into her apartment building.

Chapter Three

Talia's apartment had been tossed. Someone was clearly looking for her treatment formula and her information on recreating it. Paintings had been pulled off the walls and even the mattress in her bedroom had been removed from the bed as part of the search.

Shane had to admit he was impressed with her hiding place. He didn't call her his little brainiac for no reason. Now they had the satchel with her disks, flash drive, papers, and notebook, along with one shopping bag of personal necessities.

He wanted as few things that could potentially have been bugged with a tracker as possible. The people after her were clearly determined, and he had no way of knowing whether they'd planned this in advance, in anticipation of her completion of her work.

They could grab anything else she needed once he determined where they were going. A safe house was one possibility, but he needed more details from her first.

He'd called Ian from the road, and when they arrived at the high-rise building that housed McKay-Taggart, they met up with his boss in a conference room on the same floor as the main offices.

Ian wasn't alone. Nor was he with any of the MT crew.

"You brought the girls?" Shane asked, shocked Ian's twins were sitting at the table, coloring, but he had a hunch the quiet wouldn't last long. They were Taggarts, after all. Chaos would inevitably follow.

"Oh my God, they're adorable!" Talia exclaimed, her eyes lighting up at the sight of the children. "How old are they?"

"Five." Ian turned, and Shane realized he had his infant son strapped to a carrier attached to his chest. And there were throw-up stains on his shoulder.

"Problem?" Ian asked, cocking one eyebrow, daring him to comment. "Because if there is, you should have had your emergency during business hours."

Shane raised his hands in a gesture of peace. "No, no problem." Ian wouldn't hurt him in front of his girls, but it was prudent to stay on his boss's good side.

"Charlie's home sick," he said of his wife. "Now what's the emergency and who's the client?"

"That would be me. Talia Shaw." She extended a hand to shake.

Ian shook his head. "I'm sticky. The girls handed me their lollipops on the way in."

Shane held back a snort of laughter. Nothing relegated big, bad Ian Taggart to the status of normal human being like his family. Shane almost envied him, but he reminded himself he hadn't done marriage all that well the first time.

And as long as he was in this line of business, he wouldn't be finding a woman who could put up with the hours away from home, not to mention the danger. Amy, his ex, had been sweet but fragile, and she couldn't deal with being married to a cop. Bodyguard was no different. Although he had coworkers who'd found their significant others despite their choice of careers, Shane didn't believe it was in the cards for him.

He glanced at Talia, taking her in at the same time as Ian, and Shane knew what his boss saw. A petite woman, glasses giving her a smarty-pants air, he thought with a grin. She'd changed into a comfortable pair of body-hugging leggings at her place, a long, off-the-shoulder T-shirt, and a pair of sneakers.

Soft.

Delicate.

She wasn't Amy but she was damned close. And she needed his protection, not his lust.

"Motherfucker," Ian muttered. "It's like that?"

"Charlie said not to let you curse in front of the girls," Shane reminded him.

"Then don't drool all over the client."

Talia sucked in a surprised breath, and Shane knew his cheeks burned with embarrassment. Damn Ian and his intuition. Of course, Shane probably *was* all but drooling when he looked at Talia.

"Tell him what's going on," Shane said, changing the subject. "And now that you're safe, you have time for more detail."

He gestured to a chair and pulled it out for her to sit. Just as they all settled in, the girls, Kenzie and Kala, began to play tag around the table. And Ian ignored them.

Talia toyed with that locket around her neck and began to explain her job. "Basically it comes down to this. The drug can cure a congenital heart defect in utero. But that means the big drug companies lose tons of money providing patients with drugs over the course of their lifespan, whatever that might be. In my mother's case, it wasn't long enough," she said, looking down at her hands.

His heart clenched at her admission. He knew her history, that she'd lost her mom at a young age. Shane was lucky enough to have both parents, still happily married. He couldn't imagine such a loss, times two. Her father had passed away as well.

"It sounds to me like big pharmaceutical is somehow involved and they want to stop the cure from getting out there," Ian said, interrupting Shane's thoughts.

She nodded. "Exactly. My assistant called me in a panic, but he wasn't at the lab. Everything is gone. I'm sure they thought they acquired the entire formula, but they only have the last third. I broke it up. Part two is with us now."

"We stopped at her apartment to pick up the formula on the way here. The place had been ransacked. And I dropped a tail on the way here," Shane told Ian.

"What? You did?" Talia shook her head and sighed. "I didn't see anyone," she muttered, sounding disappointed in herself and her detecting abilities.

"Got it. How did they miss finding the formula?" Ian asked, his gaze on his girls, whose pace around the table had picked up.

"Because it was beneath the shower in a waterproof safe with her fingerprint as the entry," Shane said.

And Talia squared her shoulders with pride. So damned cute, he thought, cursing himself for the distraction from what was important.

Ian blinked, admiration crossing his face. One of the girls shrieked, and Ian cringed at the ear-piercing sound. "Keep it down. These guys don't have your daddy's ability to tune you two out," Ian said to the screaming girls.

"Whatever you say," one of the twins said dutifully, sounding exactly like—

"She gets her sarcasm from her mother," Ian said too proudly, if you asked Shane. "Okay, so back to business. Where's part one?" he asked, following both his girls and the story without missing a beat.

"My mentor. He's the one who trained me to be careful."

"Paranoid," Ian said. "But damned smart."

Talia nodded. "He started this research before he retreated to parts unknown in Oregon. I took it over. But someone stole a piece from him years ago, and he learned to take precautions."

"So you need to get to your mentor," Shane said. "And then?"

She swallowed hard. "His ex-wife, Sheila, is head of a pharmaceutical company. He can contact her and she'll make sure the formula gets into the right hands."

"You need to call him," Shane said.

She scrunched her nose at the question. "I can't."

"Explain," Ian said.

"He's eccentric. And he trusts very few people. So I have a special way of reaching him. I go to Portland and I have to put a handwritten note, myself, no postmark, not mailed, in a post office box. He comes to town the second and fourth Thursdays of the month. I can ask him to meet with me that way. He won't know to bring the research with him, but we can go back with him to get it."

Shane nodded, mentally cataloguing what would happen next, as he had to get her from here to Portland safely. He glanced at Ian. "I need a decoy when we leave here. I'm thinking Simon and Chelsea for a match in looks. Meanwhile we need to thoroughly scan and check her things before we take anything with us that could be bugged."

"Hutch!" Ian called out, and the tall, lean, bulkier now ex-hacker walked in with a piece of red licorice hanging out of his mouth.

"That was fast," Talia said, stunned.

"I called him in, figuring you'd need him. Search and scan," he said, pointing to Talia and her bags.

Shane rose out of his seat before anyone could blink or draw breath. "I'll handle Talia. You take her things."

"Motherfucker," Ian muttered again.

The girls, who'd gotten quiet again, were on Hutch in an instant, pulling at his pants. "Candy! We want candy!"

"Charlie's gonna kill me," Ian muttered as Hutch, the man with a sugar addiction, reached into his pocket and supplied the already rambunctious kids with a sugar rush they didn't need.

A little while later, Ian left, kids hanging from him as they headed home.

Hutch had handed Shane a piece of scanning equipment while he took Talia's personal belongings back to his office to handle his end of things and call Simon and Chelsea in for backup.

"Your boss is... interesting," Talia said, once they were alone.

That was a good word for Ian Taggart. "You okay?" he asked her, making sure she was on solid mental ground before they started off on their trip.

"A little overwhelmed but otherwise fine." She flashed him a bright smile he thought was forced.

"Well, I need to check you over. You know, for bugs and trackers." And there was no way in hell he'd wanted Hutch's hands anywhere near her body. The thought made him see red.

He held up the metal wand meant to search for a standard tracking device.

She rose to her feet. "What do you want me to do?" She met his gaze, trust in her eyes.

Which was pretty damned amazing given their history. One they hadn't yet addressed. He had to remain professional now and not cop a feel like he'd done when he was a kid. No matter how much he wanted to.

"Hands and feet spread wide," he said through clenched teeth.

She swallowed hard and spread her legs, then raised her arms and held them out.

He knelt down, started at her feet, and swiped the wand down her outer leg, then traveled up, from foot to inner thigh, holding his breath at how close he was to her body and her sex, wishing he could pause for further exploration, cursing himself for the inappropriate thoughts.

He slid the metal over her belly and around to her back. Up and over her curvy ass. Her breasts, noticing her nipples puckering as he breathed close. He even scanned her eyeglass frames and the locket on her neck.

By the time he finished, sweat dampened the back of his neck and he was hard as stone.

"Are you finished?" she asked breathlessly.

"Yeah." He cleared his throat and rose to his feet.

"Ready to get moving, kids?" Hutch strode back into the room and deposited her belongings on the table. "All clear on my end."

"All set here, too," Shane said.

With the details taken care of, they headed for the parking garage, where Simon and Chelsea, who'd arrived minutes before, pulled out first in a nondescript sedan. Once the decoys were on their way, Shane and Talia exited in a similar vehicle.

Each headed in opposite directions, neither one toward Portland, though Shane would eventually circle back that way when he was certain they didn't have a tail. After they were well into the trip, he could relax a little and focus more on Talia.

* * * *

Shane didn't talk much during the initial ride out of Dallas, and Talia respected his silence, knowing he was focused on making sure they left the city without anyone following them. She was too wired to relax, and it didn't help when they stopped an hour into the trip to switch cars with another agent, a safeguard Shane and Hutch had prearranged.

She wondered how her lab job had turned into such a nightmare. Even if Jonah had prepared her for just this kind of eventuality, she'd never believed anyone would come after *her*, she thought and rubbed her arms with her hands.

"Are you cold?" Shane asked, reaching to turn down the air conditioning inside the car.

"No." She shook her head. "Just wound tight," she murmured.

"I can only imagine. But you're safe. We've taken every possible precaution," he said, his voice deep and reassuring.

"I know. And I appreciate you dropping everything to help me out. I mean, after all these years, I'm basically a stranger and—"

"You're not a stranger, smarty-pants." He met her gaze through his aviators and grinned, causing her belly to twist and a jolt of desire to travel through her veins.

"No, I guess I'm not. You're Tate's best friend."

He inclined his head, eyes on the road. "Long distance aside, he's like a brother to me."

Did that make her like a sister? The thought didn't sit well with her and she wasn't surprised. When she was younger, she'd had a crush on him and had freaked out when things got too intense. Now that she was an adult, she recognized the desire he inspired in her was stronger...and not going away.

When he'd searched her earlier, the wand moving around her body parts, his face nearly between her thighs, a definite sense of arousal had pulsed through her. Her nipples had grown hard, her panties wet, and if they hadn't been in the middle of a serious situation, she might have jumped him right there.

And from the muscle she'd seen ticking in his jaw, she assumed he'd been affected by her nearness, too. Of course, that could be wishful thinking. Either way, she didn't want him to treat her like family or consider her a little sister. Because she definitely didn't feel that way about him. She never had.

"But this isn't all about Tate, is it? You're helping me and I'm grateful."

"It's my pleasure. Seriously."

She bit down on the inside of her cheek. "Okay, good." She blew out a deep breath and stared at the dry landscape through the car window.

"So how have you been?" she asked him. "I mean, we have time to talk now, right?"

"I think we're pretty safe," he said, glancing in the rearview mirror.

From his posture and general wariness, he never let his guard down, which she appreciated.

"I've been good," he said. "Working at McKay-Taggart suits me."

She could understand that. His boss was a unique man. She had a feeling the rest of the office was similarly interesting.

"But didn't you always want to be on the police force? At least that's what you told me back in high school."

He frowned, but that didn't detract from his good looks. "Back then I didn't know what being a cop would mean."

"And what's that?" she asked, curling a leg beneath her. She was intrigued by the fact that something he'd been so drawn to hadn't worked for him as an adult and was curious to know why.

"I had this case. A young girl was killed." He gripped the steering wheel tighter, his knuckles turning white under the strain. "My partner and I, we did everything by the book. Dotted the i's and crossed the t's. And in the end, the guy walked because the jury found reasonable doubt."

She winced at the outcome that had obviously hurt him so badly. "I'm sorry."

He inclined his head. "I couldn't handle the job knowing my best wasn't good enough. Protection means I can stop a threat before it hurts someone, or at least have the chance to. I get more satisfaction here than fighting the law in an attempt to get justice after the fact."

"Makes sense." She nodded, rubbing a hand along the thigh of her pants.

While she worked in a lab, she did so knowing she was trying to help people in the long run, so she understood his frustration about working within a tightly controlled system.

Time for a subject change, she decided, not that he'd like her next choice. But she couldn't help wanting to know more about him and the man he'd become.

"So… I heard from my brother you were married."

He shot her a surprised glance. "Yes. I was. It ended a couple of years ago. Amicably, as far as those things go. Amy wanted a husband she wouldn't have to worry about getting shot, maybe killed in the line of duty. And she wanted one who was home at a reasonable hour. That'd never be me."

She pursed her lips and nodded. When Tate had gone to his wedding, Talia had experienced a pang of sadness at the prospect of him being taken. Which was silly because at that point she hadn't seen Shane in years.

"Okay, time to turn the tables," he said, breaking into her thoughts. "How are you?" he asked, his shoulders finally relaxing now that the spotlight was on her.

"Other than running for my life?" she asked, wanting to keep the mood light. "I've actually been good. If you consider busy good. I've been wrapped up with my job and working the kinks out of this formula. It's been an exhilarating ride. Until today. And now I'd like to bring it to fruition. I want the drug to get to the public so it can help people as planned."

"So they don't suffer like your mother did?" he asked, his voice going soft.

She stared out the window, trying not to let sadness engulf her as it usually did when she recalled losing her mom. The slow way her body had given out along with her heart.

"Yes. So their families don't have to go through the hardships when one parent is on disability and another has to work extra hard to afford treatment." So the kids weren't at loose ends because the adults' focus was on illness and fear.

He reached over and touched her shoulder, sending a ribbon of warmth flowing through her. "I'm sorry you guys had to go through that kind of childhood."

She sighed, knowing there was so much worse. "My parents loved us." And she'd lost them too early, prompting her to guard her own heart zealously from hurt. "It just wasn't all sunshine and roses. But whose life is?"

"Still pragmatic, I see."

She grinned.

"So what about you? No marriage in your past?" he asked.

Despite the sunglasses, she could see he was getting a kick out of asking her about her personal life, and she deserved it.

"No. Like you, I work too much for any rational human being to understand. And it's not something I can see myself giving up any time soon."

"I guess we have that in common," he said.

"Besides, with love comes inevitable loss. I'd like to minimize any more pain in my life," she said, surprised she'd opened up to him that way. "I keep my relationships light."

"Too pragmatic," he muttered. She wasn't about to argue. "So I take it that means no boyfriends you're leaving behind?"

She tucked her hair behind her ear and glanced at him, wondering if this was just tit for tat conversation. Or whether there was something more behind the question.

"No. My last relationship was about a year ago." *If you could call it a relationship*, she mused, thinking back.

A colleague wanted details on her research and decided he'd sleep with her to work his way in. She hadn't even been that hurt on an emotional level, just royally pissed he'd tried to piggyback on her work.

"Interesting," he said in a gravelly voice.

Her stomach flipped in anticipation of him asking or saying

something more…something that would let her know if she was the only one experiencing this desire at such an inappropriate time. But he remained silent.

A little while passed, each alone with their thoughts, when Shane spoke.

"How about lunch?" He gestured to a sign indicating an upcoming rest area.

"Yes. Feed me, please." She pressed a hand to her empty belly.

They stopped for lunch before getting on the road again.

They talked more, revisiting some of their shared past, the tutoring she'd done with him, the fact that he'd always had a hot girl sniffing after him…but neither brought up the last time they were together. Or the kiss.

By the time they saw signs for Albuquerque, they'd been driving for over ten hours total. Her legs were cramped, her butt hurt, and she wanted nothing more than a hot shower and a warm bed.

"Are you hungry for dinner?" he asked.

"I could eat." In truth, she was starving, but she hadn't said anything since lunch. She didn't want to hold them up or be a problem when they had a timetable to stick to.

He nodded. "Me, too. And we should stop someplace where we can get a room and a good night's sleep. We'll start fresh in the morning."

"*A* room? As in one?" she blurted, immediately wishing she'd stopped the words before they'd spilled out of her mouth, because really, she didn't want to come off as a prude.

"One room, two double beds. That's as far as I'm willing to compromise and still be able to keep you safe."

She nodded, biting the inside of her cheek so she didn't speak again and say something stupid. It was bad enough she'd been an awkward teenager around him, but she was an adult now, and she didn't want him to see her as anything but a capable woman.

A sexy woman he desired might be too much to hope for. She knew herself. She attracted brainy guys. Scientists. Not hot-as-sin bodyguards like Shane.

Chapter Four

Shane picked up fast food on the way to a cheap motel, wishing he could take Talia to a nicer place and at least get her a decent meal and higher-quality lodging. But they were better off holing up at an off-the-beaten-path dive where he could see the parking lot from his window and hear if anyone came up the walkway outside.

She didn't seem to mind, which he appreciated. They ate in their room. She curled her legs beneath her on one of the beds, ignoring the ugly plaid covering, and ate quickly, devouring her food.

She was obviously hungrier than she'd let on, and he felt bad he hadn't thought to offer an extra stop.

"Next time you're hungry, say something," he instructed as he finished his burger, balled up the wrapper in his hand, and pitched it into the trash can across the room.

She paused, french fry in hand. "You know what? I will. I hate being hungry." She laughed and picked up the soda, taking a long sip.

He studied her intently. She didn't react the way he expected. To anything. She wasn't frightened and fragile, she was dealing with the situation with humor, even joking about her predicament earlier. Nor was she a panicked mess of nerves, and he had to admit, maybe she was made of sterner stuff than he'd given her credit for.

It bothered him, though, the way she spoke about relationships. A warm, giving woman like Talia shouldn't close herself off from experiencing love because she was afraid of loss. Of course, he understood where she was coming from. A teenage girl losing her mother at such a crucial age, and her father a few years after that.

He might have given up on having that in his life now, but he hadn't ruled it out forever. When he was ready to slow down or take a desk job, he figured he'd be able to open himself up to trying again. But Talia deserved to have someone to come home to at night. To take care of her, to be there for her when she needed him.

His chest ached at the thought.

Before he could think on it further, she cleared her throat, capturing his attention. "I could use a shower and that good night's sleep you mentioned." She scooped up her garbage and rose from the bed. She threw all of it in the trash.

He nodded. "I'll wait until you're out and then I'll take a quick one, too." He dug through his duffel and pulled out a stun gun. "Here. Keep this on the dresser. Just in case."

Her pretty brown eyes opened wide behind the frames. "What? No. I don't even know how to use one."

"And that's what lessons are for."

He stood beside her, breathing in her sweet scent as he walked her through the basics of use. He couldn't stop the reaction to being so close, his dick hardening in his jeans. It didn't help when she left to shower, leaving him pressing a hand against his cock to alleviate the discomfort caused by the vision of hot water running over her naked curves.

His imagination went wild with thoughts of the drops sliding over her slick body, following them with his hands, catching them with his tongue as they trailed over her dusky nipples.

He groaned, knowing it was going to be a long fucking night, sleeping in the same room and not being able to touch.

* * * *

Aware of Shane just a few feet outside the small, dingy bathroom, Talia showered and changed into a T-shirt to sleep in. She wasn't a girly girl, didn't dress up to climb into bed, and rarely had a man she needed to impress in the same room. It was too late to wish for something sexier to put on that showed off her curves, reminding herself she was on the run, not looking for sex with her hot companion. Although she had to admit, she wouldn't turn him down this time.

She drew a deep breath and stepped out of the bathroom. Shane had taken off his shirt, revealing the muscular body with tanned skin she'd seen so much of earlier that morning. Had it only been less than twelve hours ago that this crazy journey had begun, bringing Shane back into her life?

She swallowed hard. "Bathroom's all yours," she said, glancing away from his spectacular body.

"I'll be out in a few minutes."

"Take your time."

He strode into the bathroom and shut the door, turning on the water, which she already knew was tepid and weak. But that didn't stop her from envisioning him naked, as he'd been in the outdoor shower.

He'd wash himself, only this time, maybe he'd be thinking of her in the next room. And if his thoughts were going the way of hers, he'd be hard and in need of relief. He'd grip his cock in one hand and pump himself with a meaningful stroke.

She moaned out loud at the sensual notion. She shook her head and grabbed a hairbrush from the bag, pulling the bristles through her thick hair, the pain from the tugging helping her to forget the arousal ever present around Shane.

Without warning, a loud bang sounded and the entry door came crashing open. She screamed and dove to the far side of the bed as a big intruder loomed large, scanning the room. A glance and he found her, crouching low beside the furniture.

She didn't recognize the man who stalked toward her.

"Just give me what I want," he said in a too-reasonable tone.

He wanted the formula she'd put her sweat and tears into. "No way."

He reached for her at the same time she lurched backward to get away from him, her back hitting the nightstand hard.

She was trapped with nowhere to escape.

"Formula, bitch. Where is it?"

She shook her head in refusal.

He put his hands around her throat and squeezed, cutting off her airflow. Pain shot through her and spots appeared in front of her eyes.

"Feeling more cooperative now?" He eased the pressure off, hoping for an answer.

She coughed and remained silent, glaring at him defiantly. She wasn't about to give up her life's work. He squeezed his big hands tighter. Her head spun until she began to crumple against the dresser.

Suddenly he released her and she gasped for air, drawing a big, gulping breath, as she realized Shane had thrown the man off her, slamming him into the wall across from her.

Unfortunately he came up swinging.

The room still spun, but Talia pushed herself to her feet, catching sight of the Taser. She grabbed the gun. Shane swung at the man, the blow hitting his jaw, and he went down. Before he could shake it off and rise again, Talia aimed at the intruder and fired.

He jerked hard, his body in spasms, giving Shane time to rise over him and place a foot on his chest, ignoring his twitching form.

He glanced at Talia. "Grab my bag. There are zip ties at the bottom."

She pulled out the restraints, and in no time Shane had tied up the man, leaving him in flex-cuffs, writhing on the floor.

"Are you okay?" she asked Shane at the same time he asked her the same.

He came up beside her, fixing her glasses, putting them more securely in place before running his big hands gently along her sore neck. He rubbed his thumbs over her skin, causing her to shiver. His eyes were glazed with a combination of concern and anger, but his touch was so very gentle.

"I'm fine," she assured him. She was trembling, but since this ordeal had started, she'd learned quickly to adapt.

He'd shown up in time, she thought, and she exhaled a long, relieved breath.

He glanced at her, scowling as if he didn't quite believe her. Her scratchy voice might not sound great, but she'd live. And that's what mattered.

"How the hell did he find us?" he muttered, running a hand through his hair. "We must have had a tail I missed. Grab your things…" He hesitated. "No. Get dressed but leave everything you can behind. We can stop for new clothes and shit when we put miles behind us. Let's get out of here before someone comes looking for him."

"What about the bag with the formula?" she asked quietly.

"We'll put the items in my duffel. Leave the satchel itself here."

In no time, they were back on the road, her heart pounding hard in her chest.

Shane didn't show what he was feeling. He had nerves of steel as he focused on the road ahead… and behind them.

"Where are we going?" she asked.

"We'll drive toward Portland till morning. Then I'll call Ian, check in, and ditch the car at a used car lot. I also want to scan you one more time. Maybe I missed something."

His gaze alternated between the front and rearview mirror, his aggravation at being found evident.

"I'm sorry. I don't know how they tracked me." She curled into herself on the passenger seat.

"It's not your fault. As a matter of fact, you're pretty impressive under pressure." He turned toward her and smiled. "You stepped up and tased the bastard. Are you sure your neck is okay?"

"It hurts, but yeah. I'm good." She appreciated his concern.

She was glad he saw her strength, too.

* * * *

While Talia dozed beside him in the passenger seat, Shane drove north, his head full of recriminations over the fact that they'd been discovered, wondering what he'd missed. He glanced over, also marveling at the fact that Talia had stepped up.

She hadn't shrunk in the face of danger, she hadn't panicked, she'd done what she needed to do and helped save his ass in the process. Yeah, he'd have taken the guy, but she'd made it a hell of a lot easier on him.

He grinned, listening to the soft little noises she made while sleeping, her eyeglasses on her lap. A glance at the clock told him he could call the office, so he pulled a burner from the bag on the floor at Talia's feet.

Ian answered on the first ring. "Talk to me."

"We were made at the motel. Damned if I know how. I'm going to switch wheels and stop somewhere we can scan everything again. Not that I imagine we missed much. Fucking big pharmaceutical conspiracy. They could have tagged her anywhere."

"Agreed. My sources at the Dallas PD tell me Talia's assistant was found bound and gagged in a closet in the lab. Guy's petrified but otherwise fine. I don't think he's involved in any way. Unfortunately the security guard out front was taken out."

"Dead?"

"Confirmed," Ian said.

Talia popped up at his use of the word. He placed a calming hand on her thigh, and a jolt of immediate awareness hit him hard.

Her gaze met his, and she drew her tongue over her lips.

"Stay safe and keep in touch," Ian said, disconnecting the call.

"Who's dead?" Talia immediately asked.

He drew a deep breath, knowing there was no way to sugarcoat the truth. "The security guard from your lab. Your assistant was found tied up but unharmed."

If Shane had to guess, there'd been a confrontation with the guard. Her assistant had just been in the wrong place at the wrong time. Talia and her work were clearly the targets.

She flinched at the news. "That's awful." Her voice cracked and he didn't remove his hand from her leg.

"Talia, don't blame yourself." He knew the tendency would be there. "They'd want the formula no matter who created it. Greed is the root of all evil, remember."

"Yeah. It's just… I knew him. He was a nice man. He had a wife, kids. Suddenly it's just so *real*."

He turned his hand over and covered hers.

"Thanks for understanding," she said softly. "And caring."

He did care. More than he wanted to admit.

Chapter Five

Shane ditched the car, bought a used sedan, and stopped at a Target so Talia could replace the clothing and items she'd left behind. He didn't have a sister, wasn't used to shopping with women, except for the few times Amy had guilted him into coming along to the mall. Not fun.

Still, he wanted Talia to get the things she needed, so he gritted his teeth and walked into the large store, bracing himself for a long haul despite the fact that they were in a rush. To his surprise, she breezed through the aisles, picking up leggings, a pair of jeans, T-shirts, bras, and underwear, all without missing a beat or trying anything on. The toiletry trip went equally fast.

"This was much easier than I expected," he said as they reached the line for the cash register. He'd kept an eye out for trouble, but so far it was quiet.

She shrugged. "I have no time to shop, so I usually buy things online. I know my size. It was easy. Why so cynical?" she asked.

He squirmed under her perceptive gaze as they stepped closer to the register. "My ex-wife liked to go shopping and drag me along. Her idea of husband-and-wife bonding."

"I take it it wasn't your idea of a good time?"

"No." He recalled how she'd dawdled, browsing and taking her time over each purchase, oblivious to his frustration, while he'd been antsy to get home to take care of things around the house on his rare day off. She'd wanted him nearby. He'd wanted downtime alone. "We were different on so many levels."

"How'd you get together?" she asked, placing the clothes from the cart onto the conveyor belt.

"My partner's wife introduced us. We were attracted to each other. I was ready to settle down, or so I thought." He shrugged. "We didn't take the time we needed to really get to know each other."

The cashier began scanning the price tags, and they turned their attention to paying. But the words lingered in Shane's mind, because once again, he'd tried to paint Talia with Amy's personality...and was proven wrong again. It was a minor thing, but opened his eyes even more to how much he liked and admired his little brainiac.

After they'd paid, she changed in the rest room while he kept watch outside.

She opened the unisex bathroom door and poked her head outside. "All set. Everything I was wearing is in the trash."

He nodded. "Okay. Before we go, let me come in and scan you one more time." He raised the duffel he hadn't let out of his sight that held not just his necessities but the formula, as well.

She stepped back to let him in, and he slid past her, breathing in the sweet-smelling scent of her shampoo as he entered the tight space and she closed and locked the door behind him. Just a whiff of her essence had him hard.

He frowned, placing his bag on the ledge of the sink and pulling out the scanner Hutch had given him. He needed to focus on this. Keeping her safe. Not the differences between her and his ex or the way she got to him on a visceral level that had him thinking about sinking into her warm body at very inopportune times.

"Ready?"

She spread her legs wide, arms following suit. "I've assumed the position," she said on a laugh.

He chuckled and knelt down, managing an objective scan of her body, even though his eyes catalogued her full breasts beneath the thin T-shirt she wore and the tight leggings that hugged her ass and hips.

Her breath caught on an audible hitch. One that went straight to his cock.

"You're clear," he said, forcing himself to rise to his feet. As much as he was relieved, he was still uneasy. "We need to keep moving."

"I know," she said in a hoarse, too-sexy voice. Her gaze met his, distinct awareness in the clouded depths.

"So my plan is to get on the road and away from here, then pull over so I can catch some sleep."

She nodded. "Do you want me to drive?" she offered.

He shook his head. "I'm fine, but thanks."

They gathered their things and hit the road once more.

* * * *

A short while later, Shane pulled over at yet another motel, where they checked in and he settled in for a much-needed nap.

Talia was smart enough not to say a word when the motel had no double-double rooms, only one with a king-size bed. She wasn't focused on anything except getting Shane some shut-eye. And though she might have told him she'd sleep, too, she lay awake, keeping an ear and an eye out for trouble.

He'd been so steady throughout the ordeal, for her, it was the least she could do. She placed her glasses on the nightstand, turned on her side, and watched him sleep, his handsome face relaxing at last.

But he never fell into truly deep breathing. He was on alert even when he was supposed to be resting and rejuvenating.

She relaxed herself, but she didn't truly fall asleep, either, when after only a couple of hours, Shane came alert in an instant, eyes opened wide, and turned to face her.

"You're up," he said, sounding surprised.

She smiled. "Someone had to protect you while you slept," she said, gesturing to her friend, the Taser she'd put on the night table.

"Tough and smart," he said, his blue eyes twinkling.

She grinned. "And so far so good because nobody's found us."

"So either we dropped the tail or we got rid of whatever they were using to track you."

She sighed. "Or we got lucky for now and we shouldn't jinx it."

"I don't believe in luck."

She couldn't help but smile at his serious tone. "I like that you're careful."

"It's my job."

She didn't care about the reason. "Well, it makes me feel safe, and I need that right now." She propped her head in one hand. "*You* make me feel safe," she admitted.

"I do *now*."

She narrowed her gaze. "What do you mean?"

"There was a time I didn't. I know it's ridiculous all these years later, but I owe you an apology. I shouldn't have—"

"Kissed me?" she blurted out. *Shut up. Let him finish his thoughts,* she warned herself. *Hear the man out. Don't blow it for once.*

His lips turned up in a grin. "Oh, I definitely should have kissed you. I just shouldn't have tried to take it further."

"And I shouldn't have overreacted, but…it was my first time."

His gaze softened. "I figured you'd never had sex before."

Her cheeks burned, but she forced herself to correct him. "I'd never been kissed before."

His eyes opened wide in utter shock. "Oh, man. No wonder you freaked out. I had no idea." He reached out and placed his hand over hers, warm and comforting, alleviating her embarrassment somewhat.

"Why would you? You were so much more experienced than me in every way. And you were eighteen. I thought you were thanking me for helping you pass chemistry, but I didn't want my first time for more than a kiss to be out of pity."

"Pity?" He shook his head, and before she could blink, he moved near, his lips close to hers. "There was no pity in that kiss." His gaze met hers.

"But… I thought you didn't really want *me.*"

He raised an eyebrow. "You thought I didn't want you?" he repeated in obvious disbelief. "Do you still think that?"

She pulled her bottom lip into her mouth before releasing it again. His stare tracked the movement.

"I don't know," she whispered.

"I do." And before she could breathe, his lips captured hers.

A sweep of his tongue, a low groan at the first touch, and she knew. This wasn't a teenage kiss. This was hot and electric. This was everything.

His lips were soft one minute, rough and demanding the next, and for a woman with some experience but not much, she reveled in the dominating way he took control. Much the same way he'd called the shots from the minute she arrived at his house, he dictated this kiss.

His body came over hers, big and muscular. He bracketed her in heat, his heavy erection settling gloriously between her thighs. Desire swamped her, and she slid her fingers into his hair, moaning under the onslaught of emotions rushing through her. Excitement that this was finally happening, a strong yearning she'd never experienced before for any man, and disbelief that the need overwhelming her was reciprocated.

His mouth traveled a hot path down her neck, suckling on her skin. Fire licked at her veins, and she was ready for so much more, but to her disappointment, he slowed down, lifting his head and studying her.

"This is too dangerous. I'm protecting you. And I rushed things once before—"

"I'm not seventeen, Shane. I'm a woman who knows her own mind."

"And I'm the man who's supposed to keep you safe." He rolled off her and pushed himself to his feet, his shoulders stiff with tension. "We need to get back on the road if we're going to make it to Portland in time for you to contact your mentor."

She sighed but she couldn't deny the timeline. She could, however, fight his sense of duty the next time they were alone. And she intended to do just that.

* * * *

Shane brooded for the better part of the drive to their next stop, annoyed with himself for making a move on Talia. He couldn't seem to get it right with her. She was vulnerable and in need of protection, and he'd taken advantage. But was he right in his thinking? Or was he thinking more about his past with his ex than what he knew of Talia and the woman she'd become?

Clearly Talia had been a willing participant in that kiss, so maybe taking advantage wasn't really accurate. He already knew he hadn't labeled her correctly. When she'd shown up on his doorstep, knees buckling and panicked, he'd told himself she was like his ex-wife. Petite. Fragile. Afraid.

But what had he seen since? Strength of character. Someone who didn't buckle under pressure, who held her own with an attacker, who didn't give away the information they wanted in exchange for her safety. She'd even tased the guy before Shane could take him down and kept watch over him while he slept.

So clearly he not only needed to reassess his characterization of his smarty-pants, he had to stop comparing her with his ex. And cut himself some slack for wanting her.

Around eight p.m., he pulled off the exit and drove around until he found a roadside bar where they could eat dinner, and if his app was correct, there was a motel a half mile down the road where they could spend the night. No car had followed him or been behind him for miles, so he felt safe enough stopping here.

Talia had dozed off again, and he gently shook her awake. "Rise and shine. Time to eat."

She popped up quickly at the mention of food, causing him to laugh. He liked a woman who appreciated a good meal, and from the time they'd gotten on the road, Talia hadn't eaten one salad, which was amazing considering her petite, albeit curvy frame.

From the amount of cars in the gravel parking lot, the restaurant was obviously busy.

"Looks like we found a popular place," she said.

As long as he could get them in and out safely should the need arise, he'd make it work. The place was old and beat-up-looking, but it was the best he could do under the circumstances.

Despite the number of people, they were lucky enough to get a table immediately, as most of the crowd was hanging out around the bar and near a dance floor.

The hostess, a young girl in a cowboy hat and a perky smile, seated them.

"It's so rustic," Talia murmured as she slid into her chair. "I kind of like it."

He shook his head, amused. He should have realized by now Talia was one to make things pretty damned easy considering their situation.

They settled in to their seats and studied the menu, which offered some pretty basic fare. Shane didn't mind.

"Can I take your order?" A waitress arrived at their table, a pad in hand.

"Talia?" He gestured for her to go first.

"You go. I'm not sure yet," she murmured.

"The barbeque chicken sounds good. And a Diet Coke." His stomach growled at the mention of the food, but the music was loud, so nobody noticed.

"I'll have the same," Talia said. "Thank you."

The waitress took the menus and left them alone.

"It feels so good to get out of the car." With a low, sexy groan,

Talia stretched beneath the table, her foot rubbing up against his leg.

The gesture and sound were innocent, but his body's reaction wasn't. His cock perked up in his pants. Not that his dick was ever unaware with Talia around.

"Agreed," he said, shifting and adjusting himself discreetly beneath the table.

After sitting in close quarters with her for hours, smelling her fruity shampoo, watching her alternate between making cute noises when she slept and entertaining him with stories of people in her lab when the silence became too much, he was very much aware of her.

Not to mention the kiss that was always playing in the back of his mind, on a never-ending loop. Mocking him for being an idiot and ending things before either of them found any true satisfaction.

It had just been a prelude. A tease. And he wanted more.

"Aww, look." She pointed to an older couple who had risen from their seats and were walking hand in hand to the small dance floor, which was crowded with people. "That's so sweet," Talia said as the woman put her head against the man's chest.

He mentally added romantic to her list of attributes. "They remind me of my parents," he said, grinning as he watched them.

"You're lucky and so are they." Her eyes misted as she took in the slow movements of the older couple.

His heart twisted in his chest as he realized the things she'd missed out on in life. The things he took for granted. Parents who not only grew old together but who, by example, proved that happily-ever-afters did happen. Maybe not for him, but he didn't not believe they could occur.

He glanced over. Her eyes had filled up, misting with tears. "I just miss her still. I think I feel an ache for the events she missed out on in my life…graduations, jobs, celebrations. She'd be so happy about this cure. Not for herself, but—"

"She'd be proud of you." He smiled because *he* was proud of her. "So would your dad."

She brushed at a stray tear. "I know." She smiled. "Hey…let's dance," she said, clearly wanting to change the subject.

Before he could answer, she rose from her chair and grabbed his hand, pulling him to join her.

He gave in…only because he would have an eye on the front and back doors the whole time. She slipped into his arms like she was meant for him, her breasts pressed enticingly against his chest, causing his body to hum with desire. A burning need for this one woman.

And when she slid her hands into the back pockets of his jeans and cupped his ass, all bets were off. He wrapped an arm around her waist, lifted her until she was up on her toes, and sealed his lips over hers. He felt her mouth curve up in a smile. Little smarty-pants had gotten what she wanted, but in doing so, he'd won as well.

He slid his tongue between her lips and delved deep, indulging in her sweetness and taste, his cock pulsing against his jeans and her soft body. They swayed in time to the music, her tongue gliding against his, his mind wondering how fast he could get her out of here and into a bed.

"Food," she whispered, breaking the kiss. "We need to eat so we can get out of here."

She was reading his mind. "I could devour *you*," he said, nipping at her bottom lip.

Now that he'd overanalyzed for the better part of the day, he was finished treating her with kid gloves, as if she were some fragile flower. This woman had guts and strength, and he wanted her bad.

After they got through this meal and he checked them in for the night, he wasn't backing off once they were alone. He'd be careful with her safety, but he was giving in to what they both wanted.

He grasped her hand and led her back to the table, where their plates were waiting. He barely tasted his food, eating only as a means to keep up his strength—they were both going to need and appreciate it later.

"This is good barbeque sauce," she said, her eyes glittering as she ran her tongue over her lips. "Hot and spicy." Her cheeks flushed a healthy pink.

He knew it wasn't in her nature to be the sexual aggressor, but she was pushing him anyway. Even if it wasn't easy.

"You're stepping up your game." And she was getting to him. He gestured for the check.

She lifted her shoulder in a delicate shrug. "You didn't give me much of a choice. You weren't going to make the first move. Or the next one. And we're long overdue for this, wouldn't you say?"

He reached into his pocket and threw cash on the table, pulled her from her seat, and made a beeline for the door, his body hot, bothered, and insisting that he get her alone.

Except as he pushed through the crowd, the back of his neck began to tingle, and a glance at the front entrance told him why. A man stood at the entryway, looking out of place in black slacks and a white shirt, a holstered gun covered by his jacket but visible by the slight bump of fabric.

And though this guy could be anyone, Shane never ignored his sixth sense. But fuck. How the hell had they been located again?

He pulled Talia behind a group of people, out of sight.

"What's wrong?" she asked, taking his cues and inserting herself into the crowd.

"We're going out the back. Take off your glasses," he instructed Talia. "Just until we get to the car." They were less likely to recognize her without the visible prop.

She slid her glasses off her face and tucked them into her hand. "I don't get it," she said, her frustration mirroring his own.

"Let's figure it out once we're out of here. Stick close." He glanced around and saw the man walk up to the hostess stand, which was far from the dance floor, giving them the opportunity to slip away.

He kept to the perimeter, making their way toward the back door by the restrooms. They ran for the car and were on their way before the guy realized he'd missed her.

"What the fuck?" he said, banging his hand against the steering wheel. "How do they keep finding us?"

He glanced at her just as she lifted a hand, rubbing the locket around her neck, a nervous gesture she made a habit out of doing when she was upset. "I've scanned that thing," he muttered.

"What?"

"The locket. I've scanned it three times now. I hate to say it, but you're going to have to toss the necklace." He slowed and pulled over to the side of the dark road. "Out the window. Do it now." He hit the electric button and her window went down.

"What? No! It belonged to my mother!" She rubbed the heart possessively, her long fingers touching the gold piece. "I can't give it up." She placed a hand on her own button, and the window slid closed.

Frustration warred with a heavy dose of sympathy, made even more relevant because of the conversation they'd had and her admission about how much she missed her mom. Unfortunately it was compassion he couldn't afford if he was going to do his job.

"Talia, if somehow they tagged the necklace, we have to unload it to keep you safe."

Tears formed in her eyes as she hung on to the precious piece. "It's the one thing I have of my mother's. You can't possibly expect me to throw it away."

He groaned, rubbing a hand over his face. He hated putting her in this position, but he couldn't see an alternative. "If it was morning, I'd put it in a safe deposit box at a bank or open a post office box and leave it there, but it's after business hours. I don't know of any other way to drop the tail."

The only shot she had of keeping the jewelry was if whoever was after her never had the opportunity to get their hands on it. He met her gaze. "Do you ever take it off?" he asked.

She blinked, answering without thinking it through. "Of course I do. I leave it on my dresser when I shower."

He doubted anyone had been in while she was there. "Do you always wear it to work?"

Meeting his gaze, she shook her head.

"So they could have gotten into your apartment and tagged it without you knowing."

A tear dripped from her eyes as she nodded.

Then, she took him by surprise, lifting her hands to the back of her neck and unhooking the clasp. "Dad gave this to me after Mom died. He said she'd want me to have it…to remember her by."

She drew a deep breath. "But I don't need a *thing* to keep my memories alive." She curled her hands around the chain, the locket dangling from her hand, and she pressed her lips to the heart. "I have her in here." She touched her chest.

His own heart ached watching her.

Then she opened the window and tossed the heart out, turning away. "Let's go." She closed the window, squeezing her eyes shut tight.

"Talia," he said gruffly. "I'm sorry."

She didn't reply.

He put the car in drive and pulled back onto the road.

Chapter Six

Talia's heart hurt. Although she'd lost her mother a long time ago, being forced to throw away her last tangible link was unexpected. And painful. She hadn't let herself feel much of anything since running from the lab, but now she wasn't just sad, she was also angry.

She turned to Shane as he put the car in park in the lot of a hotel an hour away from the one they'd originally planned on staying in.

She hadn't spoken to him since he'd told her to ditch her necklace because she'd needed time to think. "I don't blame *you*," she said. "I'm upset at the circumstances that forced me to have to throw away something that meant a lot to me."

She'd lost her mom and she had plenty of good memories of her mother to warm her heart, but she'd always felt that the locket connected her to her mom. She was going to have to make do with what she remembered and hold those memories close.

Shane faced her, his expression somber. "I know. And I'm sorry."

She believed him. She sensed he understood how difficult that act had been for her. She didn't think he'd made the demand to throw it away lightly. And despite what had just happened, and the time that had passed since leaving the restaurant, she didn't want to lose the momentum of desire that had played out between them earlier.

She didn't break eye contact, wanting to convey the fact that she wasn't holding on to her sadness or anger, at least not for tonight. Not with him. And the longer their gazes held, the more that warm, heated feeling began to return.

Earlier she'd cracked Shane's protective exterior and reached the hot-blooded man beneath. The academic types she usually dated didn't go all caveman, dragging her out of a restaurant, planning to head to the nearest motel for sex. And though it hadn't worked out that way, she had to admit, she'd liked the feeling of knowing he wanted her as badly as she desired him.

He wouldn't push her now. Knowing Shane, he'd assume she needed time, and she would have to make the first move.

She reached out and touched his cheek, rubbing her palm against his scruff. "I still want you."

He let out a low grumble, grasped her wrist, and placed a kiss against her hand. "Let's get a room," he said in a gruff voice.

"Yes, let's." Her heart beat hard in her chest. Harder than when she'd realized she was alone and on the run and for a much more exciting reason.

He approached the front desk of the run-down motel, where a sleepy-eyed clerk glanced up at them with disinterest. "Yeah?"

"One room, king-size bed," Shane said, pulling out cash to cover the cost up front.

The guy behind the desk passed the key over the counter. "One-fifteen around back."

Shane kept a firm grip on her hand, and despite the awareness thrumming between them, she sensed his heightened attention to their surroundings as they parked the car behind the motel and walked to their room.

"Looks quiet," he said, putting the key in the door and ushering them inside. "But I'm not taking any chances this time."

She toed off her shoes while he immediately locked the door and braced a chair against the knob.

"Good." She didn't want any interruptions. What she wanted was Shane's intense focus on her.

She slid her tongue along her lips and strode over to where he stood, watching her. His eyes glittered with darkened desire and intent.

"You're sure?" he asked her.

She inclined her head. "Need me to grab your ass again? You know I'm big on providing scientific proof."

"Very cute," he said with a grin, relaxing now that they were locked in the room.

She wasn't sure where her bravery was coming from, but knowing he desired her allowed her to feel freer than she had before. The fact that they were on the run meant her adrenaline levels had been spiked for days. And the thought of sweaty, hot sex to take the edge off sounded like a glorious idea. Getting a second chance with Shane sounded even better.

He met her by the side of the bed. Standing close, he looked into her eyes, then removed her glasses, placing them on the nightstand. There was something inherently sexy in that move, and her heart beat so hard in her chest she thought she could hear the sound. She figured *he* could hear it.

He reached for the hem of her shirt and pulled it over her head, revealing a plain beige bra. She hadn't bought anything frilly at Target, but he obviously didn't care what her underwear looked like, because his eyes glittered with heated passion.

He unhooked the back clasp and slid the garment down her arms, dropping it to the floor. His gaze settled on her bare breasts and tightened nipples.

"Fucking perfect," he said, eyes darkening at the sight.

Her cheeks flushed under his scrutiny. She'd never been the recipient of such a slow, deliberate seduction. He took his time, not just stripping her out of her clothing but looking his fill. Letting her know he was pleased with what he saw. He deliberately stroked his knuckles over her nipples, and she trembled, the buds beading into hardened peaks, and her panties grew soaked, her body swaying toward his.

He knelt then, pulling her leggings and underwear down together, waiting as she stepped out of her clothing. "God, you smell good," he said in a gruff voice. "You want me."

"I do." She shook with need, beyond the ability to be embarrassed at his frank words, as she stood bare in front of him.

Rising, he cupped her face in his hand and kissed her slowly, gently, his tongue swirling around inside her mouth, parrying with hers. She needed his hard, hot body pressing into her, skin to skin, and she lifted his shirt, intending to make that happen, but he broke the kiss, stripping quickly. As eager to get himself naked as she was.

She had no time to appreciate his tanned, muscular chest because he undid his jeans and stripped, kicking them aside. Her gaze fell to his thick erection jutting out from between his thighs, a light coating of pre-cum on the head.

He wrapped a hand around his length and groaned, gliding it back and forth in a forceful pump. She had the sudden desire to touch him. To drop to her knees and taste. To revel in finally being naked with this man.

"On the bed," he said, striding over to his small duffel and returning with a foil packet in his hand.

She wasn't about to argue and pulled down the spread so she could climb onto the clean sheets. He sheathed himself and joined her, the mattress dipping under his weight.

"I waited a long time for this," he said, his words causing an unexpected rush of joy to spread through her.

"Me, too."

"One problem," he murmured, stroking her cheek. "You're the kind of woman who deserves slow and sweet. But given the circumstances, we need to move quickly so I can be aware and alert. Slow is going to have to wait for next time," he said, easing his body over hers.

He was already talking about next time.

She was primed for now. "You don't hear me complaining."

His thighs covered hers, his cock nestled into her sex, and her entire body came alive.

She reached for him, but he was in control, grabbing her hands in his and raising them above her head. Then, cock in his free hand, he slid the head through her damp folds, setting alight every nerve ending she had. Her stomach rippled with need, her core clenching with the desire to be filled.

"Hang on," he said, notching himself at her opening and easing inside.

She groaned at the invasion, his thickness parting her, taking her over. She raised her hips, pulling him in farther, feeling every inch fill her up.

"Fuck. You feel so good." He shook and she marveled at the fact that she could affect this big man on such a primal level.

Pulling her hands free, she grasped his shoulders so she could hold on. With every thrust of his hips, waves of pleasure pummeled at her, and she scored her nails down his back, barely recognizing the noise in the room as coming from her.

He glided in and out, her inner walls softening, accepting him so deep with each pass. He was hard, fast, and the way their bodies meshed was sheer bliss.

He kissed her then, his mouth and tongue matching the motion of their hips, and she was lost. Sensation took over. She clenched her sex, clamping his cock deep inside her.

"Perfection," he muttered, sliding a hand between them, his finger pressing on exactly the right spot. Glorious contractions began, her orgasm starting immediately from the combination of the angle he hit inside her and the delicious rotation of his finger against her clit.

"Oh, Shane." She trembled as her climax hit and she fell apart, losing all sense of time and place as she came apart in his arms. He followed immediately after, taking his pleasure in her body, thrusting in and out until he collapsed on top of her, his breath hard and hot in her ear.

Chapter Seven

Talia woke up feeling sore in the best possible way. She didn't have a single regret about last night. How many people received second chances? It wasn't like they were talking about forever, something she didn't believe in, anyway. Even her parents, as in love as they were, had their lives cut short. People died. Left. It was better to keep things casual, and that was what she had with Shane. No matter how fantastic the sex or how much she liked and admired him, this was a passing fling.

Besides, they lived very different lives, his a fast-paced rush of adrenaline in his line of work for McKay-Taggart, and hers with long hours in the lab. Neither of them had time for relationships. His job had cost him his marriage. No matter how much she enjoyed his company, no matter how her feelings for him were continuing to grow, she had to remember reality. And act accordingly.

She ought to look to his actions now, as well. Shane was all business as they rushed their individual showers—because he insisted they didn't have time for him to get distracted by her naked body—and though she didn't sense he had any misgivings, he wasn't getting all soft and mushy, either.

They gathered their things and hit the road, agreeing to stop for gas and food at the first place they came across.

When they finally reached Portland, the first order of business was to leave the handwritten note asking Jonah to meet up with them tomorrow at a nearby Starbucks. She knew he'd pick up the mail at four p.m. on the dot and would be there for her in the morning, after which they'd be close to ending this nightmare. Which meant the end of her time with Shane.

She pushed the depressing thought aside, because at that moment, Shane pulled into the parking lot of a glittering high-rise hotel.

"We're staying here?" she asked. It was so much nicer than any place they'd been able to find so far.

"I think you've earned a night in a decent bed without worrying about security, don't you?" he asked, a grin lifting his sexy lips.

"Why do I suspect you'll still be worrying?" she asked.

"Because that's my job. But I can assure you nobody's going to be breaking down your door. And Ian's got connections with people he trusts to get us a room. It's all good."

"I am not going to complain." They exited the car, leaving it with the valet, the only choice, and strode into the lobby.

The hotel was a far cry from the roadside motels they'd stayed in up until now, and Talia took in the mirrored and gold-plated walls, crystal chandeliers, and marble floors. She knew this was a five-star hotel, and if it meant her safety and it gave Shane a night to relax a little, she was all for the expense.

Check-in was easy, as promised. Ian had already arranged for the room on the lowest floor, giving them a stairwell escape route should it become necessary.

Once in the room, he locked the door and flipped the security bar, a bonus they hadn't had in previous places.

She took in the king-sized bed, something Shane had requested and received, and grinned. She knew they'd make good use of the large mattress. The one thing she'd discovered was that she and her bodyguard were extremely sexually compatible. That was a big deal she'd never truly had with another man. Sex? Yes. Explosive orgasms? No.

Speaking of orgasms, there was no point in wasting this luxury. She glanced over her shoulder at Shane, who'd put his bag on the bed and was studying the room. So intent. It was time for him to relax.

"We can eat in the restaurant downstairs," he said, planning ahead as always. "Or order in room service."

"Either sounds good, but I think I'd like a shower first. Wash off the grimy feeling of being in the car for hours." She bit down on her lower lip. "Care to join me?" she asked in her most provocative voice.

His gaze darkened at the suggestion. "I think that can be arranged," he said in a husky voice.

She pulled her shirt over her head and walked to the bathroom, feeling the heat of his gaze on her back as she walked.

The bathroom was large and luxurious, spa products set up on the countertop and in the open shower with the overhead rain showerhead. She turned on the water and undressed the rest of the way, stepping underneath. The warm drops cascaded over her. She felt so good and tipped her head back, washed and conditioned her hair, and was rinsing it out when she felt the heat of Shane's body as he joined her.

He stepped in, coming up behind her and wrapping his arms around her, his big hands cupping her breasts.

"Mmm." She leaned her head back against his shoulder and sighed in aroused delight.

She wondered what it would be like to have this kind of time with Shane without the pressure of being followed and on the run. For the next two days, at least, they could pretend there was no one else around.

He reached for a small bottle on the shelf and poured a nice amount of scented liquid into his hand before returning to his task. Now soapy, he lathered her body. Starting with her breasts, he took the time to cup the full mounds in his hands and pluck her nipples with his fingertips, rolling them around, causing waves of desire to ripple through her.

Her sex clenched with yearning, and she turned in his arms. He backed her against the wall, kissing her hard, his hand sliding down her side, her hip, and around to her stomach. His fingers dipped downward, gliding through her folds, her sex damp, and not just from the water. His fingertips were rough and felt good against her slick flesh.

One finger penetrated her, and she sucked in a shallow breath. He added a second, and she tipped her head, hitting it on the wall behind her. But she couldn't focus on that slight pain when the incredible sensations being delivered were so intense. Every pump of his fingers hit a sweet spot inside her, and pleasure built quickly, white sparks of desire flickering behind her eyes.

"You're going to come and I'm going to watch," he said in a gruff tone, his voice a turn-on along with his words.

She so was.

She just didn't expect what came next. He dropped to his knees, braced his hands on her thighs, and buried his face between her legs. His tongue lashed her clit. Over and over, he licked, sucked, and teased the nub with his teeth, soothing again with his tongue. She grasped his head, pulling at his hair, while at the same time holding him in place, never wanting the powerful sensations to end.

She gasped, panted, and lost all sense of time and place as the sudden orgasm overtook her, bringing her up and over the edge. She cried out, invoking his name, God's name, and a host of other things she couldn't recall by the time she sagged against the wall, dazed and satisfied.

But he wasn't. He rose and slid his lips over hers, letting her taste herself on his tongue before breaking the kiss.

"I don't know about you, but I'm ready for a soft bed." He shut off the shower before facing her once more.

He grabbed a towel and dried her off, then took care of himself, quickly and efficiently. He dropped the towel and swung her into his arms.

She clasped her hands around his neck and laughed. "Shane!"

He grinned as he deposited her on the bed and came down over her, his heavy erection pulsing against her belly, pressing deliciously against her clit, sending ripples of awareness through her veins. Arousal had awakened inside her again, her sex wet and ready for him.

"Are you going to get a condom?" she asked.

He dipped his head and let out a groan. "We used what I had on me. Fuck."

She blew out a shaky breath. "I get shots," she said, meeting his gaze. "It's just simpler for me."

His blue eyes turned serious and intense. "You're sure?"

"For you? Yes." He didn't need to know that she never had sex without a condom or that she trusted he wouldn't do something reckless and put her at risk. His honor was one of the things she admired about him. Even after all this time, she knew he wouldn't hurt her.

He nodded, his jaw clenched, as he took in the implications of her suggestion. This would change things between them on a deep level neither could take back.

"Are we good?" she asked shakily.

"Yes. Do you want to know why?"

She nodded, running her hands over his damp hair.

"Because that means I'm going to feel every sweet inch of you," he replied, bracing his arms on either side of the bed and pushing himself into her in one swift thrust.

She certainly felt every last inch of him. She arched her back, pulling him deeper, clenching around him, and delighting in the waves of desire that overtook her.

This felt different. *He* felt different. Raw, powerful…and meaningful, she thought and moaned as he slid out, only to drive back in with a loud groan.

"God, you feel incredible," he muttered, rocking into her, sensually, slowly, when she'd expected another hard, fast taking.

He placed his arms on either side of her and pushed himself up as he continued his passionate assault on all of her senses.

He smelled good, his skin felt hot beneath her hands, and she was lost in sensation, so when her orgasm came, it came differently than before. She was swept away in an incredible wave of pleasure that took her higher and carried her over into pure bliss.

* * * *

In a complete one-eighty, Talia fell fast asleep right after sex and Shane lay awake thinking. Because that…that had been…something else.

Talia was something else.

He'd always known she was different. And if he was a different kind of man, he'd be thinking more serious thoughts about his little brainiac.

In their short time together, she'd blasted through the wall he'd erected since his divorce. He wasn't worried about her fragility because she'd more than proven herself strong and capable. She didn't panic. She wasn't afraid. She stood up for what she'd worked so hard for. And she was a woman who knew her own mind, understood what she wanted out of her career. Out of her life.

In another time or place, she'd be his perfect woman. But nothing could change the fact that he was a man always in dangerous situations, rarely home, and she was a woman who deserved commitment. A man who'd be there for her at the end of the day.

Of course, she didn't want that kind of relationship. What was it she'd said?

With love comes inevitable loss. I'd like to minimize any more pain in my life. I keep my relationships light.

He could relate to the sentiment…even if, looking at her, he wished things were different. For both of them.

He shouldn't have been surprised he'd gone from another chance to sleep with this woman to thinking such serious thoughts.

This was Talia, after all. The girl he'd had a thing for when he'd been too young and stupid to know what to do with her, how to take care of her better. He knew now. And no matter how fast his heart beat around her, no matter how much he enjoyed her or wanted her in his life, that was a lesson he'd learned. How to put others before himself. How to put her first.

So he'd get her to her professor friend, figure out how to keep her formula safe, and go back to the life he knew. He had no business considering relationships. At all. No matter how much a part of him wanted to.

* * * *

Dinner in the downstairs restaurant consisted of the most delicious steak meal Talia had ever had. A juicy filet, creamed spinach, a baked potato loaded with sour cream and she was in food heaven.

Shane was alert and wary, but he'd also relaxed enough to enjoy both her company and the food.

"Dessert," a waiter said, placing the cheesecake Talia had ordered in front of her.

She cut a piece and tasted it immediately, groaning at the flavor as it melted in her mouth. "This is so good."

Shane eyed her, an amused smile on his face.

"What?" she asked, laughing. "I worked up an appetite earlier." She pointedly referred to their session in the shower. And in the bed.

His eyes heated at the reminder. "I just enjoy watching you eat."

"Want a bite?" She scooped a piece onto her fork and held it out for him.

He shook his head. "No sweets for me." He paused, a killer smile edging his lips. "Except for you. Then I'll let myself indulge."

She laughed, as amused as she was secretly thrilled by his comment. "I see. So that's how you keep that killer body." She nodded in approval.

At the compliment, he sat up a little straighter in his chair. "Are you trying to get me to drag you back to the room again?"

She twirled the fork in her hand. "I wouldn't object," she

murmured, only partly teasing.

He glanced up, his gaze catching the waiter's. "Check, please."

* * * *

Shane walked by Talia's side, keeping an eye out for anyone suspicious-looking…but he didn't see anything to alert him. Which didn't mean he'd let his guard down. Although her locket had seemed like the obvious choice for a bug, that was almost too easy. His gut didn't like the odds that they'd lost the people following her or their ability to track Talia.

Once back in the room, he double locked the door and put a finger over his lips, indicating she shouldn't talk just yet. He headed straight for his bag and began a thorough scan of the room and all likely places a bug could have been placed while they were at dinner.

Large pharmaceutical companies had big money at their disposal. A maid or a front desk clerk could be bribed to let someone into the room and search for the formula…which they'd kept with them during dinner.

While Talia watched, bottom lip pulled between her teeth, Shane worked his way around the room. When he reached the bed, he ran the wand around the headboard, and damned if he didn't get a loud beep when he scanned the main piece.

He patted behind the wooden board and found the sucker, pinned to the back. *Fuck*. He held up the small bug and placed a hand over his mouth, indicating she should be quiet.

So it hadn't been the locket, he thought in frustration. She'd dumped the memento for no reason, and it was his fault. Guilt gripped him hard, but he needed to handle *this* situation before he could deal with their emotions.

He left the offending bug on the dresser, grabbed Talia's hand, and led her to the bathroom, where he ran the shower for extra noise.

"Don't panic," he said, looking into her wide eyes as he spoke in hushed tones.

"They broke into our room while we were at dinner?" she asked, appalled.

"Probably paid someone to let them in," he said. "But that doesn't explain how they keep finding us." He scowled, frustrated that they'd gotten the better of him at every turn.

She shrugged. "I'm at a loss, too. But it wasn't the locket," she whispered, sad at the memory of what she'd had to leave behind.

His gut twisted as realization dawned for her that she'd thrown away her last link to her mother for no reason. "I'm sorry."

"It's not your fault. Let's just focus on what we can control. What do we do now?" she asked about the bug.

"I have an idea."

She straightened her shoulders, bucking up as she always did, and he was so damned proud of her in this moment.

"I'm listening."

He spoke in a low whisper. "We're going to go back out there and lay out our plans for tomorrow, except we're going to lead them somewhere else completely."

He pulled out his cell and began to search hospital names in the area. "We don't want them near Dr. Goodwin, so you're going to mention that we're meeting him here." He showed her the name of a medical center on the other side of town.

Shane wasn't convinced the ruse would take care of the problem, however, because these assholes had managed to catch up with them every time.

She blinked in surprise. "What if they follow us anyway?" she asked, her brain following the same line as his.

"We're going to specifically mention that you don't have the whole formula, the man you're meeting does, but it won't be with him." He didn't want to set Goodwin up as an immediate target, either.

Hopefully the plan would buy them time to meet with the good doctor, drive to the cabin, get their hands on the rest of the cure, and turn it over to Dr. Goodwin's ex-wife.

"Once we have a location where your mentor lives, I'll call Ian, and he'll send a team to have our backs. Just in case."

She visibly swallowed hard. "Okay."

He grasped her forearms in a sign of reassurance. "Ready?"

She nodded.

Grabbing her hand, he led her back to the bedroom, standing by the bug. "You're sure there's no way to contact your mentor faster?" he asked. He gave a squeeze of her palm to let her know to answer.

"I can't. He's eccentric. He already knows to meet us at Providence Portland Medical Center, where he has an office. Hopefully he has the rest of the formula with him there."

He winked at her, mouthing, *good job*. He deliberately gave a loud yawn. "I want to turn in early. I'm exhausted. You wore me out," he said with a laugh.

She narrowed her gaze.

He placed a finger over his mouth and gestured to the bathroom again, where they could talk in private.

She followed him into the room and turned on the shower.

"What's going on?" she asked in a whisper.

"I don't want to sleep in here. We'll get another room and come back in the morning to shower before we head out. No reason to be aware of a bug all night. We'll be up tossing and turning. Let's just go back out there, make some noise, and pretend to go to sleep. Then we'll sneak out again."

She nodded, eyes lit up at his plan. "Sounds like a good idea to me."

Acting on impulse, he leaned over and pressed a kiss on her lips.

Just because he wanted to.

Chapter Eight

In the morning, he checked in with Ian, then they proceeded with the next part of their plan. Shane was relying on the bug and the people who'd planted it and had been listening to their conversation to head in the direction of the hospital, but he also knew there was every chance they had at least one guy with eyes on Talia. The fact that she didn't have the entire cure in her possession and they now knew it, however, would definitely buy them time to get to the cabin. Because the people after her would wait for her to lead them to the remaining pieces of the formula.

Meeting in a public place with plenty of people around would prevent anything dangerous from happening. At least that was his hope. Considering he hadn't a clue how they kept tracking Talia, he was wary of taking anything for granted.

Not with Talia's safety at stake.

They sat inside the coffee shop with a view of the window and the sidewalk outside, waiting for Jonah Goodwin. He wrapped his hand around a warm coffee cup, his second of the morning.

"It's been years since I've seen Jonah," Talia said, taking a sip of her latte.

"Were you close?" he asked, wondering about the relationships in her life.

"He was my professor in medical school." She smiled at what must be a good memory. "He drove students crazy with his erratic schedule, requirements, and theories. But I liked him immediately. He took me under his wing." She shrugged. "Got me my current position because I wanted to follow in his footsteps and work on the cure for what my mother had."

Her eyes suddenly lit up. "Oh! Here he is!"

Shane turned to catch sight of an older man who looked just as Shane had pictured for a reclusive eccentric. His hair was to his shoulders and bushy, his face covered in a grayish-white beard. His jeans were old and faded, a plaid flannel shirt covering a T-shirt. And probably because he hadn't expected this urgent meeting, he kept looking over his shoulder and glancing around.

He stepped inside and Talia shot out of her seat. "Jonah!"

The big man swept her into a hug, confirming their close relationship despite not having seen each other in a while.

He ended the embrace and met her gaze. "Who's this?" He gestured to Shane, who was hovering protectively nearby.

Talia stepped back. "This is Shane Landon, my bodyguard."

Goodwin narrowed his gaze. "You need protection? What's going on?" he asked without acknowledging Shane or shaking his hand.

"Let's sit," Talia suggested. She gestured to the table and chairs behind them.

He pulled out a seat and settled into it. Shane and Talia did the same.

"Talk to me," Jonah said, never truly relaxing.

"Okay, so the good news is that Christopher and I were finally successful in working out the right treatment. We were ready to go into the testing phase, and the company knew it. Next thing I know, someone wiped my lab clean, took the computers and equipment, and I'm sure they assumed they'd gotten the whole formula. Of course, they didn't."

"Because you listened to me and broke up your results," he said, nodding as he took in her story.

She rubbed her palms against her leggings. "Someone's been after me ever since. They want the rest of the formula."

"And the only reason for that to happen is if someone wants to keep the medicine from ever getting to market." He rubbed his beard thoughtfully. "You have your part?"

"Right here." Shane patted the duffel he hadn't let out of his sight.

"And I assume you have a plan?"

Shane leaned in. "It requires your trust."

"And you can trust Shane," Talia assured the older man. "I've known him practically my whole life."

Jonah scowled. "I don't trust anyone. Well, very few people, anyway. But if he's kept you safe, he has my thanks. What do you need from me?"

Shane leaned closer to the older man. "We need the first part of the formula. And that means we need to go with you to your cabin," Shane said. "Look, I work for McKay-Taggart Security in Dallas."

"I've heard of them," Jonah said, his facial expression less harsh now that he thought Shane was legit.

"Eventually whoever's after Talia is going to realize I sent them in the wrong direction this morning or they have someone following Talia. Either way, we might have a tail as we go to your cabin." Shane placed a hand behind Talia's chair, his fingers brushing against her back as he spoke to the doctor.

"I want to give my people your address and set a trap for whoever's been after her," Shane explained. "The cops can take over dealing with the bastards from there."

"And the formula?" Jonah asked.

Talia placed a hand on the man's forearm. "I want you to reach out to Sheila. If we can get this into her hands, her company can take over from here."

Jonah shifted uncomfortably in his seat. "I haven't spoken to her in a while."

"I don't believe she hasn't tried to reach out?" Talia pressed. "The only reason you two aren't together is because you decided withdrawing from life was what you wanted."

"Yeah, I hear from her," he muttered.

She blew out a long, relieved breath.

"Good. So can you call her and set things in motion?" Shane said. "Because we'll need to transfer the formula to her quickly. Call her and—"

He shook his head. "I don't have her number memorized."

"Of course not," Shane said. "Just take out your cell and—"

Talia cleared her throat. "He doesn't have a cell phone."

"Excuse me?" Surely Shane had heard wrong.

Jonah shrugged. "I don't like extra equipment on me. Nobody needs to reach me, and if they do, they know how." He tipped his head toward Talia, as if to say, *you see? She found me.*

"Fuck me." Shane rubbed a hand over his face. "Guess we'll handle that when we get to your cabin. Can I at least have the cabin's address to send to McKay-Taggart so we can set up an op?" he asked the eccentric man. "Otherwise we're going up there with no backup, and trust me when I tell you, somehow they will figure out how to tail us. They've been one step ahead of us the entire time."

Talia frowned at the reminder. "He's scanned me. We tossed my mother's locket. I don't know how else they've tracked me."

"Hmm." Jonah narrowed his gaze, rubbing his beard thoughtfully. "You get your annuals shots at the lab? Flu? Birth control? Anything like that?"

She nodded, her eyes wide. "What are you saying?" she asked, but from the dawning awareness in her eyes, she was beginning to figure it out, Shane thought.

"That they injected you with a tracker, the bastards," Jonah said.

"What?" she asked, horrified.

Shane's feelings were about the same. "Motherfuckers. And we'd never find it with a basic scanner."

Jonah spread his hands wide as he explained. "An RFID chip injected under the skin that can be used to track you. You have a problem with one of the shots? It take longer, or something hurt that shouldn't have?"

She managed a slow nod. "Yes. My hip was sore for a while after the flu shot this past November."

"If you even got a flu shot," Jonah muttered.

"Those bastards! This is such a violation!" Talia's cheeks flushed red. "And to think I threw out my mother's locket for no good reason." Tears of frustration filled her eyes. "Get it out."

"What?" Shane asked.

"Get it out now." She began scratching at her hip where she must have had her injections.

He threaded his fingers through hers. "Talia, we're in public, not to mention it's going to hurt. It needs to be done by a professional. A doctor. Not me."

"I want it out," she insisted, chin lifted in stubborn determination.

Shit. He glanced at Jonah, silently pleading with him to back up what he was saying.

"Girl knows what she wants. She always did. That's why I admire her. I can't remove it myself though." He held up his hands, which Shane now realized held a fine but noticeable tremor. "But I can walk you through how to do it."

So much for backing him up, Shane thought in frustration.

He pressed his palms against his eyes. "You do realize that as soon as it's out, they're going to know we've figured out their game?" He was already calculating their strategy. "That means we get right on the road and head to the cabin. They'll find the tracker where we leave it. Then we just have to hope no one's following you as an extra precaution." But he wasn't holding out hope.

He'd just have his team meet them there.

"So you'll do it?" she asked him hopefully.

Shane inclined his head. "You're not giving me a choice. Besides, we don't want to lead them to the formula before we can get it or a copy of it to safety. We at least want a head start. We just need to move fast."

She expelled a harsh breath, then clasped her hand tight in his. "I'm okay," she whispered, more to herself than to him.

But she didn't let go of his hand, and he was grateful to be her rock when she needed it.

He turned to Jonah. "Cabin address? Please?" he added, because he sensed the older man was not comfortable sharing his personal information.

"Fine." He rattled off the address and directions, which included off-road markers and indicators he'd put in himself. Because he was that far off the grid.

"But whoever's following you can't come in by car because I have a booby trap set up that'll disable their vehicle."

"What kind of trap?" Shane asked.

"You know those spikes they have at rental car companies? The ones that require signs that say Do Not Back Up Severe Tire Damage?"

"Yes?" Talia asked warily.

"Well, those are set to activate unless it's me coming through with my remote to deactivate them first." He shrugged as if it were completely normal. "A man can't be too careful."

Or paranoid. Jesus. "Can my guys get in by helo?" Shane asked, knowing Ian was going to shit a brick at the cost because there was no way Shane was letting any of this become a billable expense.

As far as Shane was concerned, this was personal.

Jonah nodded. "Just watch out for my trees. But we'll get those bastards," he said, suddenly warming to the idea. The man was nothing if not mercurial.

But Shane couldn't worry about the good doctor. He had his own issues to deal with, and those included removing a tracker from beneath Talia's skin. And Shane was not looking forward to hurting her. Not for any reason.

* * * *

Immediately after leaving Starbucks, Shane called Ian with the cabin coordinates and address. Unfortunately the team was over a good four hours out. If they were lucky. Which meant he was on his own.

At Target, Shane and Talia picked up supplies so he could at least sterilize her skin and complete the chip removal as carefully and safely as possible. Then they locked themselves in a family bathroom. Jonah, meanwhile, said he had an errand to run and would meet them back at the spot they'd left the car in the parking lot, to lead the way to his cabin.

The bathroom was small, but not as tiny as a stall, and there was no chance of anyone walking in on them. Talia hadn't said a word since they'd locked themselves in, and Shane was too busy giving himself a pep talk about the upcoming *surgery* to have a conversation.

With shaking hands, he opened the bag of supplies and laid a pair of scissors, small razor blade, alcohol, and gauze pads on the counter. Bandages followed.

"I don't want to do this," he muttered, not for the first time.

"Come on. You've seen bullet wounds, right? It'll be fine," she said, her voice about as steady as his hands.

He shook his head, his admiration for her rising exponentially with every passing minute. "You're badass, Ms. Smarty-Pants."

She grinned. "Desperate times and all that."

She drew a deep breath and pulled the waistband of her pants down to her knees. Looking down, she patted the muscled area below her hip, near her buttocks. "Son of a bitch. Here." She grabbed his fingertip and pressed it against her flesh where a tiny raised area could be felt but not seen.

He nodded, breaking into a sweat. Was he really going to do this?

He was. He washed his hands with antibacterial soap, then doused the small blade in alcohol.

"Why don't you sit?" That way, if it hurt, she wouldn't pass out from a standing position.

Nausea filled him, but he knew the faster he worked, the better off they'd both be.

She sat, her side facing him, her hands in tight fists.

"Keep breathing," he told her.

She managed a short nod. "Just do it."

He drew a steadying breath. With the blade, he made a tiny cut, pressing down hard enough to break skin.

She sucked in a breath. Let out a squeak of pain, her real noises being held back, he knew. He swallowed a wave of nausea and kept working.

Going on and methodically following Jonah's instructions, Shane parted the skin and, using sterilized tweezers, dug in. He wasn't a surgeon, and he had to dig around more than he'd have liked, the soft noises coming from the back of her throat piercing his heart.

"Got it." Finally he pulled out the rice-sized chip, holding it up for her to see before dropping it into the towel he'd placed on the counter.

"Thank God," she muttered, tears in her eyes.

He wasn't sure how long he'd worked or how much time had passed. He'd only been aware of the task in front of him and the sounds of her heavy breathing mixed with his own.

"Okay?" he asked her.

She gave a short nod.

He did his best to close the wound with butterfly strips, determined to get her to a doctor, and probably a tetanus shot and antibiotics, as soon as they were safe.

She ducked her head, pulling in deep breaths, as he turned back to the sink and washed off the blood. He had a hunch he'd see that nightmare in his sleep often in the coming days. He cleaned up after himself, leaving no trace behind, except what he tossed in the trash. Let the bastards dig through the garbage to find their tracker.

Shane placed a hand on her shaking back. "Hey. Are you really okay?"

She met his gaze, her eyes glassy and her cheeks flushed, but she managed a nod.

Damn, she was brave. They had to get the hell out of here, but he took a minute to lift her up and pull her into his arms. He needed the embrace as much as she did. He'd never done anything like that on someone he cared about, and his stomach was roiling.

"You did good," he said, not wanting to let her go but knowing they needed to leave.

She tipped her head back. "You did better." She grinned.

Unable to resist, he kissed her lips. Not for long—they had no time to spare—but he needed a taste.

"Take the ibuprofen and we'll get on the road." He pressed another kiss, this one to her forehead.

She tore open the pain killer they'd bought and swallowed it with water. "Ready." She took a step on her foot, wincing as she walked.

He grabbed his bag, which carried everything, including the formula, wrapped an arm around her, and rushed out to the car.

They followed Jonah to the cabin in a beat-up Jeep in silence. Talia wasn't in a chatty mood, and Shane wasn't about to push her to talk after what she'd been through.

He didn't mention it to her, but they had a tail a far distance away. He wasn't surprised; they'd obviously had someone on her, and with or without the tracker, they were on to them.

Shane had known he'd have to deal with whomever was after her at some point. Better to be aware than wondering.

But no matter how you sliced it, his team was four hours away by private jet, then they'd have to take a helicopter to reach the cabin.

They were talking hours before they could possibly feel safe, and though they might all reach the cabin at the same time, there was more of a likelihood Shane would have to take on at least the guy in the car and whatever backup he'd called on his own.

Chapter Nine

Talia's hip hurt like a son of a bitch, the ibuprofen not even touching the pain, but she gritted her teeth and didn't complain. There'd be plenty of time to get medical attention once they survived this mess.

They reached the cabin four hours later, just as rain came pouring down. They rushed inside, locked the doors, and set the alarm, Jonah re-securing the trap he had set along the path to the cabin. Although the man was paranoid, in this case, his suspicious nature would help buy time, because according to Shane, Ian and his team were still fifteen minutes out.

"I don't want to alarm anyone, but we had a tail on the way here," he said as Jonah settled in front of his state-of-the-art security system. "He didn't follow us once we turned off the main road to the cabin. My hunch is he's waiting for backup."

"Oh God." Nausea lodged in her throat. "Did you reach Sheila yet?" she asked Jonah. She had to get the formula to someone she could trust.

"Negative." He kept an eye on the screens for the intruder. Or intruders. Who knew what they were in for?

She sighed. "We need to get it into her hands. And in a way that can't be intercepted. Can't you just send the formula itself via email?"

"Not until I'm sure nobody else checks her account. She's never been as safety conscious as me, no matter how hard I tried to teach her the benefits of being extra careful."

Shane, meanwhile, muttered under his breath, pacing as he ran a hand along the back of his neck. She didn't have to ask him what was wrong. Her stomach was jumping with nerves, as well.

She called her brother, checking in and explaining their current situation. Tate was worried but glad she was still with Shane, and he trusted Ian Taggart and his team, and Talia took comfort in that. Still, at this point, it was a race to see if the helicopter arrived with reinforcements before the guy who'd followed her decided to make his move, demanding the formula.

The plan was for Shane and Ian to take Talia to Sheila so Talia could turn over the formula in person. Of course, that assumed they could reach her and set up a meeting place.

Shane walked over and placed a hand on her shoulders. "How are you?" he asked, his breath warm in her ear.

"Good."

"Liar," he whispered, his fingers massaging the tight knots in her muscles.

"Okay, in pain." She didn't want him to feel guilty. "It had to be done. I wasn't going to walk around knowing my every movement was being tracked like I'm some animal."

He nodded. "I know. Look, when we get out of this mess—"

She didn't know what he planned to say, and Jonah interrupted them anyway.

"We've got company."

Shane pulled out his gun and stalked to where Jonah watched the screen. A black sedan had turned onto the unpaved path.

"That's the car," Shane said.

Jonah hit a button and reset the spikes he'd turned off for their approach, so they would spring up as a car passed, ripping apart any tires that dared to pass.

"What is he working on that he needs this kind of protection?" Shane asked, not for the first time. But Jonah hadn't answered him the first go-round.

He wouldn't reply now.

And he didn't.

The car slowed before hitting the blades, coming to a stop. A solo man in the sedan appeared to be talking into a cell phone before he climbed out of the car and began to approach by foot in the pouring rain.

"He probably called for backup," Shane muttered. He hit a button on his own cell and checked in with Ian. "How far out?" he asked.

"Patience, grasshopper," Ian said. "Ten and counting."

Shane headed to his bag and returned with the Taser Talia had grown too comfortable with. "Here."

"But—"

"I'm going to head him off outside. I don't want him getting anywhere near you, the doc, or the formula."

"Stay here until Ian arrives." She grabbed his arm, not wanting him in any extra danger because of her.

"I can't do that." He pulled her into a quick kiss, one that didn't last nearly long enough, before handing her the Taser gun. "Best case, I neutralize him and Ian arrives before his buddies get here."

She didn't want to ask about the worst-case scenario.

Shane headed out into the rain.

Her heart in her throat, Talia ran back to the monitors, where Jonah was watching. Shane stealthily worked his way from tree to tree, moving toward the entrance to the property. In another screen, she viewed the man coming toward him. They were destined to meet up, and Talia was so nervous she had to lower herself into a chair, her hand on the Taser gun.

Just in case.

"Your man's got the right moves," Jonah said.

"I just wish backup would get here." Her hand went to the locket that wasn't there, an old habit she'd have to break. But she didn't have time to dwell on it, because as she watched, Shane barreled into the intruder, dragging him to the ground.

Talia braced her hands on the desktop and leaned closer, panic filling her as the two men grappled for purchase in the damp earth. Shane was bigger, broader, and got more than his share of hits in, eventually able to knock the man down.

Shane pulled his gun just as Jonah spoke. "Problem. We've got penetration on the western quadrant of the property."

"I'm sorry?"

"Men coming in on foot from the side. A lot of them."

"What? No!" She glanced at the screen.

Shane had hauled the man to his feet and was slowly marching him toward the house, gun trained on his back as they moved. She didn't know where the other men would intercept him, and there was nothing she could do to prevent it.

Nausea and worry for Shane filled her, as did complete panic for her work if the team they'd sent in breached the house. "They can't get their hands on the formula."

For the last half-dozen years, she'd been singularly focused on this cure. To lose it now, have a big pharmaceutical company, if that was who really was behind this, bury her findings... She couldn't let that happen. Although she was tempted to run into danger herself to warn Shane, her intellectual instincts won out. There was nothing she could do to help him. She had to trust in his ability to take care of himself.

"I need your piece of the formula and access to your computer," she said to Jonah. One part was in Shane's duffel bag, and the last part was recent enough that she could recreate it from memory. At least enough to upload.

"What's your plan?" her mentor asked.

"I'm going to cut the enemy off at the knees by uploading the cure to MedFree, an open source software site." A reputable site owned by a cadre of scientists who could not be bought by big pharmaceuticals. Any reputable researcher knew the name.

Jonah didn't argue. He obviously saw the wisdom of her plan. Expose the formula so the company after her couldn't profit and remove the need to come after the cure.

He swiveled his chair toward yet another screen and typed in a password. "Here you go. Do your worst." He glanced at the monitors. "But do it fast."

She swallowed hard as Shane found himself surrounded. He dropped his gun and raised his hands in the air, outnumbered by the incoming men.

"Oh my God," she said, scrambling for the computer just as Jonah handed her two separate notebooks, each opened to the right set of information.

She pulled up the site and logged in. And then she frantically but carefully began to type.

She was still inputting the information when the door burst open wide, followed by a gust of wind. Just as she pressed the final entry and hit upload, Shane, wet and muddy, stepped inside, hands in the air, followed by what looked like an army of men in black.

"Hands in the air," one of the men said.

Fear pulsed through her, but she complied, as did Jonah.

"I want the formula," the first man through the door said, his voice deep and formidable.

"You're too late," she said, facing them. "I uploaded all the pertinent information necessary to recreate the cure onto freeware. The world has access to the formula." She raised her chin. If she was going down, she was going down having done the right thing.

Before the man in charge could reply, the sound of windows shattering echoed through the room.

"Get down!" Shane shouted.

Everything happened in a blur. A large body slammed her to the floor, knocking her breath out of her lungs. Shots rang out around her, and she heard screams—before realizing the sounds were coming from her.

* * * *

"Clear!"

At the sound of Ian's voice, Shane eased himself off Talia and helped her to a sitting position. Her face was pale, her eyes wide, her teeth chattering.

Gunshots could do that to a civilian, and he pulled her close as she recovered from the shock of Ian and the team coming in through the windows. They now had the men surrounded at gunpoint.

Jonah climbed out from beneath the desk. "Who's going to pay for this mess?" he asked, grumbling.

Ian met Shane's gaze. "All good?"

"You took long enough," Shane muttered. He'd been outnumbered and had seen them walk in and train a gun on Talia.

"You try flying in this God-awful weather. Your girl okay?"

Before he could answer, Talia struggled to a standing position. "I'm fine. Thank you for getting here," she said, ignoring her still-trembling limbs.

"The formula's safe?" Ian asked.

She rubbed her hands up and down her arms. "It's available to whomever can get it to the FDA the fastest. I uploaded it to a freeware site to prevent anyone who could profit from its destruction from accessing it first."

She sounded shocked by her actions, and Shane understood. The cure wouldn't be sold in a traditional sale from her employer to a big pharmaceutical company. "You killed your company's chance at a big sale."

"And I won't be able to guide a team of scientists into testing and see my product helping people firsthand." She sucked in her bottom lip. "On the other hand, now scientists and even hobbyists will have the chance to work with my research," she said, sounding more hopeful. "They could possibly even expand on it."

"And there will be competition to market—competition that might take your discoveries to a higher level," Ian offered.

"Regardless, what you did was selfless and brave," Shane said, completely in awe. He slid his hand into hers. "I'm proud of you." For more than just outsmarting the people after her. She'd faced down the men with guns like the brave woman she was.

She managed a shaky smile. "Thank you."

"Okay, kids," Ian said. "The local cops are coming in to clean up this mess. With any luck, they'll find out who was behind this. We're out." He glanced at Shane. "You know how much I hate dealing with bureaucratic shit."

Shane rolled his eyes. They'd all be tied up late answering questions, but Talia was safe. Which meant this particular job was complete.

Chapter Ten

Talia and Shane were separated as soon as the local sheriff and his men arrived wanting answers, considering they had bullet holes everywhere and a few non-life-threatening injuries to the men after her. Shane had refused to leave her, but the sheriff demanded their individual stories, so they'd separated. Talia was more than happy to provide her version of events.

The sheriff planned to get in contact with Dallas authorities so they could compare notes and tie up loose ends on both sides. Talia knew it would take more time and investigation before the truth of what happened finally came out.

After an hour of questioning, the men who weren't sent off with police escorts by ambulance were rounded up and taken into custody. The end of her short nightmare had finally come, and Talia couldn't be more relieved.

Shane and Talia were allowed to leave with Ian by helicopter to the nearest airport, at which point they'd fly to Dallas. The rest of his men had dispersed using Shane's car. Weight limits prohibited adding more people on the helicopter, and Shane wanted Talia back in Dallas at a local hospital near home. She wasn't about to argue. The pain in her hip had only gotten worse, especially after she'd been thrown to the floor to avoid flying bullets.

She took her first helicopter ride and was mesmerized by the feel and sights around her. With Ian around, she and Shane had no time to talk—not that she knew what to say beyond *thanks for saving me* and *good-bye*. She had no illusions about any kind of future for them. No sooner had her situation been wrapped up than Ian engaged Shane in conversation about an emergency case that had just come their way. Soon he'd be busy with his bodyguard business…as it should be.

She wondered how her company played into people wanting to steal her work. No doubt, there was big money involved and high stakes for either developing her formula or burying it for good. Her goal was and always would be to be back in a lab, doing her work. She didn't know or want any other way of life.

And if Sheila and her company could somehow get involved in the cure Talia had uploaded today, she was hoping Jonah's ex-wife would let her be involved in bringing the drug to market. Talia had sacrificed too much of her life to the cause, and she desperately wanted to be a part of its future.

An exhausting number of hours later, she arrived at the hospital, where a doctor cleaned out Talia's wound while lecturing Shane on the dangers of a civilian playing surgeon.

The poor man didn't need the reprimand. She knew he felt bad enough already. And she'd have the scar to remember him by even when he was gone from her life. The scar would be even larger because the doctor needed to go in and clean out the wound before closing it up again.

At least this time she'd had a local anesthetic to dull the pain. Not that the needles on the local had been fun, but she'd survived the ordeal. It helped that she had Shane by her side, holding her hand while the doctor worked.

Finally, the doctor, an older man with salt-and-pepper hair, snapped off his surgical gloves and tossed them in the trash. "I'll be right back with your discharge papers and prescription for a painkiller and antibiotic."

"Thank you," Talia murmured.

"You're welcome." He pushed past the curtain and walked out.

Shane braced an arm on the top of the propped-up bed behind her. "Are you okay?"

She nodded. "I am."

He leaned in close. She wanted to memorize every line and curve of his handsome face for when she wouldn't see him every day.

"You amazed me every step of the way," he said, pride in his voice.

She laughed. "I have to admit I amazed myself. Shows you what you can do when you have no other choice."

"It shows you're strong and resilient."

She brushed a hand down his scruffy cheek. "Maybe that's because I had a protector I could rely on."

"Or maybe it's because you're stronger than you think or give yourself credit for." His smile reached his eyes and warmed her heart. "Talia—"

Whatever he was going to say was cut off by the ring of his cell phone. He straightened and reached for the phone in his pocket. "Landon."

He listened and his relaxed features morphed into a frustrated frown. "Okay, yeah. I'll be there." He disconnected the call and met Talia's gaze. "Ian's calling an emergency meeting. New client."

"Okay." She schooled her face into a mask of understanding, not wanting him to see the disappointment in her expression.

Not that she didn't understand. She'd be a hypocrite if she had a problem with him taking off for work. She just hadn't thought their time together would come to such an abrupt end. Then again, she hadn't thought about it at all.

Oh, she'd told herself it would happen, but feeling the separation was something different altogether. Still, she'd known him leaving was inevitable.

"Thank Ian again for me. And you know where to bill me." Although that helicopter was going to kill her budget.

Shane grinned. "Don't worry. I think I can get you the friends and family discount," he said, as if reading her mind.

Friends. Well, it was as good as it was going to get between them now, she thought.

He leaned down and swept a kiss over her lips, lingering for too brief a time but long enough for her to inhale his scent and taste him once more.

He straightened and looked at her, his expression unreadable. "Can I call someone to take you home?" he asked.

She drew her tongue over her lips and gave his question some thought. Her brother was coming home tonight, and she didn't want to explain her situation to anyone. She could take a cab but... "I don't have my phone and I used all my spare cash. Can you lend me some money for a cab?" she asked, feeling herself blush. She knew anything she'd purchased while on the run, Ian would probably bill her for.

He frowned and pulled cash out of his wallet, handing her a good amount. "I'm sorry I have to bail on you. I wish—"

She reached out and placed her hand over his mouth, silencing him. "It's fine. *I'm* fine." She smiled, although her stomach was in knots.

A part of her wished he'd just leave already and not draw out what was hurting her more than she'd imagined. She had an unexpected lump in her throat, and though she was the most independent woman she knew, heading home alone after this adventure wouldn't be easy. A part of her was more shaken up than she wanted to admit to Shane. Or to herself. Maybe that was why he hadn't asked for his Taser gun back.

"See you, Ms. Smarty-Pants," he said, winked at her, then turned and walked through the curtain and out of her life.

* * * *

Two weeks passed, during which Talia spent a lot of time repeating her story to the Dallas PD while they discovered the fact that her company, Newton Laboratories, had been directly involved in stopping the cure from getting to market. The conspiracy between them and a big pharmaceutical company who was willing to pay to keep the drug buried went all the way up to the top, from Talia's boss to the CEO of Newton. They'd all been working together with an agreement to share in the profits of the existing drugs treating the condition for the duration of a patient's life. A much more lucrative proposition. Talia would have to testify if it came to trial, but she was hoping the men involved would take a plea.

As for her own life, she was waiting to hear from Sheila on whether her company was going to get involved in bringing the cure to the FDA. Either way, she had accepted a job offer and was due to start on the first of next month. Meanwhile, she had time on her hands.

And with that time came the inevitable thoughts about Shane and their days on the road. She hadn't heard from him and assumed he was either on the job he'd been called away for or he'd moved on to another assignment.

Moved on from her.

And wasn't that what she wanted? Time alone to work? To enjoy her solitary life? But when had words like *alone* and *solitary* bothered her the way they did now?

She ran a hand through her hair and returned to folding the laundry, no longer finding satisfaction in finishing the chores around the house. It wasn't that she missed the danger from her time with Shane.

She missed him.

She told herself the feeling would pass. That once she returned to work, she'd have no time to be emotionally down and lonely. She'd fall back into the comfort of routine and the excitement and challenge of the lab, where she'd always found satisfaction.

Her doorbell rang, and she dropped her nightshirt into the laundry basket, grateful for the reprieve, and headed downstairs to answer it.

She opened the door to find her brother on the other side. They looked alike with their dark brown hair and similar features, and today he was dressed in a pair of cargo shorts and a T-shirt. Totally casual.

"Surprise!" Tate said, pulling her into a big hug.

She squeezed him back. "What are you doing here?" she asked.

She'd seen him since her return. He'd shown up on her doorstep, coming to Dallas before going home to New York. He'd wanted to see for himself that she'd survived her ordeal intact. He was an awesome big brother.

But it wasn't like him to just show up in town without calling first.

"You sounded down last time we talked, and I knew you had some time off, so I figured I would surprise you with a short visit."

She squealed in excitement. "I'm so glad you're here."

She looked around but didn't see any bags. "Where's your carry-on?" She knew he traveled light.

"I didn't want to intrude on your privacy. I figured I'd stay in a hotel, and I already checked in and got rid of the luggage."

"Silly. You know you can stay here." She pulled him inside and shut the door behind him.

"Can I get you a drink?" she offered.

"Do you have a beer?"

She grinned. "From your last visit, I do."

He followed her to the kitchen, a sunny room with stainless appliances and light-wood cabinets. He turned the chair around and straddled it while she picked out two bottles.

Why not join him?

A few minutes later, they were each enjoying a cold brew. "Are you looking forward to getting back to work?" he asked.

She settled into the chair across from him. "You have no idea how much! I miss being busy." She wrapped her hands around the bottle, cold with condensation.

"Is that all you miss?" he asked, tipping the bottle back so he could take a long sip.

She narrowed her gaze, annoyed he wouldn't just be direct with her. "Why don't you just say what you mean?"

Tate placed the beer on the Formica table. "Do you miss Shane?" He met her gaze with his direct one.

Tate wasn't that much older, but he'd always been able to pry a secret out of her, and on his last visit, she'd admitted something had happened between her and his best friend. She'd never tell him details, and he wouldn't want to know, but he hadn't been surprised they'd gotten together in some way.

"What makes you say that?" she asked, being deliberately dense.

He rolled his eyes. "Apart from the fact that I hear it in your voice, I know you. You've had a thing for Shane for years." Before she could argue, he held up a hand. "And vice versa. I saw it in high school when you tutored him, and more recently I could tell by the way he'd ask about you...and you'd avoid questioning me about him."

She frowned. "Who knew I was obvious?" she muttered.

"Only to someone who loves you...and knows you both well."

She paused for a small sip of beer, savoring the malty taste. "It was a casual thing," she murmured, lying to herself...as well as to him.

"Was it?"

She lowered the bottle to the table. "It had to be," she whispered.

"Why?"

Aside from the fact that she'd never had a serious relationship? That she was afraid of losing people she loved? "I have no time in my life for someone who needs my attention." She was a workaholic and enjoyed that aspect of her life.

Tate shrugged. "Neither does he. And yet I have a hunch he'd be happy to spend what little free time he does have with you."

She swallowed hard. "Did Shane actually say that?" She hated the hope in her voice.

Tate laughed at her obvious interest. "He didn't have to. He's been short-tempered and a pain in the ass. Very unlike himself. Just like you've been down. Unlike yourself."

"I've been out of work," she argued as her lame excuse. She didn't even believe it herself.

He groaned. "You two getting together has been a long time coming. You've always liked him. God knows I don't want specifics about your time with him, but you haven't been yourself since you came home. Don't you think you owe it to yourself to find out if you two could actually be a couple?"

She and Shane. A couple?

She really hadn't given it any thought, had pushed all possibilities out of her mind, because aside from the obvious obstacles—their busy lives and jobs—she had a deep, ingrained fear of loss.

"What if something happens to him on the job? If he gets hurt or, God forbid, killed?" she asked, her throat feeling heavy at the prospect.

"Hey." He reached across the table and grabbed her hand. "We lost Mom and Dad, but we have each other. And you can't live every day waiting to lose the people you care about," he said, understanding like she knew he would. "Besides, what if something happened and you two weren't together? Wouldn't you regret not taking advantage of the time you could have had?"

She pursed her lips in a pout. "Just when did you get so smart?" she asked her big brother.

He snickered at the question. "I've always been intelligent. You just never liked to give me credit. So. Are you going to take my advice and go for it?" he asked.

She didn't know if it was as simple as he made it out to be. She'd have to be the one to approach Shane and risk putting her heart out there for him to crush if he didn't want the same thing.

She shivered at the very scary prospect. But wasn't it scarier to really let him go?

"I'll think about it," she promised, knowing she wouldn't be able to concentrate on anything else.

* * * *

Shane's mood matched his appearance. Foul. He was exhausted since wrapping up his latest case last night and spending hours calming a hysterical client. All he wanted to do was go home, shower, crawl into bed, and not come out for a solid week. Because his mood had been shit long before this past assignment. Since walking out of Talia's hospital cubicle, to be exact. But who was counting?

He stared around the empty conference room, waiting for his boss to join him, and he didn't have to wait long.

Ian joined him a few minutes later. "Hey, thanks for coming in," Ian said.

"What's up? Because I'm fucking exhausted."

Ian studied him, his face a mask of disgust. "No wonder clients are complaining about your mood."

"Are they really?" Shane asked, suddenly concerned his job was at stake because he hadn't been able to get walking out on Talia out of his mind.

Or how easily she'd let him go.

He ran a hand through his too-long hair and glanced at Ian.

"No, not really. Although your coworkers think you're a pain in the ass. Want to talk about it?" Ian made a gagging sound following the offer.

Shane choked back a laugh. "Wouldn't want you to exert your feminine side."

Ian rolled back his shoulders. "I don't have a feminine side, asshole. What I do have is a woman in my life, something you don't. So if you want some of my wisdom, now's the time to ask."

Shane scrubbed a hand down his face, lowering himself into the nearest chair. "After my divorce, I told myself a relationship wouldn't work with this kind of job. I travel, I'm in danger often, and my ex was too damned fragile to handle both. She wanted me around and safe. So I figured when I'm finished with bodyguard work, maybe it'll be time for a relationship."

"Let me guess. Then you met up with Talia again. I could have saved you the aggravation and told you not to fight it from the beginning."

"Why didn't you then?" Shane asked.

"What fun would that be?" Ian slapped him on the shoulder. "Seriously, some things a man has to experience for himself. You wouldn't have believed me unless you were forced to walk away and feel like you were missing a part of yourself."

Shane reeled at the accurate description. Ian had nailed his feelings on the head. Abandoning Talia had left him hollow. Like she'd taken the part of him that enjoyed life.

"And as for what she needs in a man, she seems like she handled danger just fine," Ian noted. "And from what I've heard of her in our investigations of the mess she was in, she's a workaholic. She's not going to be sitting, wringing her hands, and waiting for you to come home."

All valid points, Shane thought, his mood looking up for the first time in weeks.

"So I hope you've gotten your shit together and are ready to tell her how you feel," Ian said.

Shane glanced down at his clothes, wrinkled from a long flight and the plane grime he wanted to wash away. "I wouldn't mind a shower first," he muttered.

"Too bad, because she's waiting out front." Ian grinned, looking altogether pleased with himself.

"Excuse me? Talia's here? And you've been shooting the shit in here with me?" Shane shook his head. The way his boss's thinking worked boggled the mind.

"I had to make sure I had you in the right headspace before meeting up with her. See, she met Charlie and my wife likes her. I promised Charlie I'd prep you so you didn't do anything stupid."

Talia was here. Shane had stopped listening to anything Ian had said beyond that.

"I'll send her in. Don't fuck it up," Ian said, and walked out the door.

* * * *

Talia did as she'd promised her brother. She'd given a lot of thought to a relationship with Shane. She considered what she wanted out of her life and what she was willing to give of herself. Because it wasn't fair to ask him to get involved when she wasn't willing to invest herself, too.

Being forced to look inward wasn't easy, and she didn't like what she'd learned. Because she dove into work for all the right…and wrong reasons. It was right that she wanted to find a cure for what had ultimately taken her mother from her. It was right that she'd dedicated her life to a cause. But it was wrong that she buried herself and her feelings and needs because she was afraid of more loss.

She'd essentially lost Shane when he'd walked out of her life almost three weeks ago, and she hadn't had a good day since, so she knew what she had to do.

She rubbed her hands together nervously. She hadn't wanted to show up on Shane's doorstep only to find he wasn't home, so she'd called McKay-Taggart to ask when he'd be in the office. Her call had been transferred directly to Ian, which surprised her, and he'd been almost gleefully willing to help. He'd called her this morning, letting her know Shane was back in the office.

So here she was, following Ian down the hall. He paused at the entrance of the same conference room where this had all begun. "Go easy on him," Ian said, a grin on his face.

Who knew the big man liked to play matchmaker? "Thank you," she said, drawing a deep breath before she gathered her courage and stepped inside.

Shane stood at the window overlooking the outdoors. "Hi," she said, and he turned to face her.

She was surprised by his appearance—the scruffy beard, the exhaustion in his eyes, and the rumpled wrinkles in his clothes, dark jeans, and a light blue polo shirt. She drank him in, his face just as handsome, the scruff adding to his sex appeal. And she couldn't care less about the wrinkles.

"Hi," she said, feeling suddenly shy but knowing that wouldn't work for why she was here.

"Hey." He shoved his hands into the front pockets of his jeans. "How have you been?"

"Good." She swallowed hard. "No, that's a lie. Not good. Not even close."

He narrowed his gaze, worry in his gorgeous blue eyes. "Did you get an infection from where I had to cut you?" he asked.

"No, nothing like that. I healed just fine. In fact, you could probably be a surgeon in your next life."

Relief crossed his features. "Good. Then what's wrong?"

It was now or never, she thought, crossing the room to where he stood. "I'll tell you what's wrong. I missed you," she said, cupping his face in her hands and pulling him down so she could press her lips to his.

He groaned, his hand coming around the back of her neck, his palm pulling her into him as he opened his mouth and slid his tongue inside in an act of pure possession. If she'd had any questions whether her feelings were reciprocated, they were gone in that instant.

He lifted her and she wrapped her legs around his waist, kissing him with everything she had, drinking in his familiar scent, his taste, all she'd missed for the last couple of weeks.

He lifted his head, pressing one more kiss on her lips and allowing her to slide back to the floor. The hard press of his groin sent sparks of awareness shooting through her body.

"I missed you, too," he said.

Her heart skipped a beat at his words. "We need to talk about where that leaves us. What do we do about these crazy feelings we have when our lives are so…"

"Busy?" he asked.

She nodded.

"First question. The danger I face doesn't bother you? You can handle my job?" he asked, sounding like he dreaded her answer.

She didn't have to think to answer. "Of course, I hate it. Who wants the person they love to be in danger?" No sooner had the words come out than she panicked.

Talk about too much too soon. Blurting things out again. Things she hadn't given any thought to. "I'm sorry. Don't freak out. I didn't mean—"

"You better have meant it," he said on a low growl.

She blinked in surprise. "I didn't just send you running?"

"Hell, no. Will the potential danger I'm in send you running?"

She shook her head. "Just because I don't like it doesn't mean I don't respect what you do. Or think you're good at it. It feeds your soul…just like my profession feeds mine. Which brings us to the next question. Finding time to be together." She pulled her bottom lip into her mouth, worried this issue would be their deal breaker.

"Well, not all my assignments are long-distance, and I've earned enough seniority with Ian to turn things down on occasion."

He raised his eyebrows in a challenge, and she couldn't help but grin. "I'll see your turning down assignments and agree to try not to take my work home all the time and to take weekends off when you're in town."

He braced his hands on her hips. "Look at us negotiating a relationship like mature adults. You know, I never wanted to be home the same way when I was married before."

She knew the admission wasn't an easy one. "It's hard to make things work when both people aren't invested in the outcome."

He rolled his shoulders, his discomfort clear. "I never realized it before. I always blamed the fact that I worked, that my job was dangerous, that Amy couldn't handle it. I guess I was partially to blame."

She brushed her hand over his scruffy cheek. "I like it," she said, laughing. "But seriously, life is about changing and growing."

"And meeting the person you love. The one who completes you." He grasped her wrist, rubbing his thumb over the pulse point she knew was jumping at his touch. At his words. At the idea of *them*. "You do that for me, Talia Shaw. I think I've been waiting for you all along."

She smiled wide. "Well, I promise you, I'm going to make it worth the wait."

Epilogue

One Year Later

Shane shifted from foot to foot in his dress shoes that matched his tuxedo, anxious for the ceremony to begin. Above him was an arch of white flowers, and in front of him, the long aisle he was waiting for Talia to walk down.

They'd opted for a small wedding, although Talia still wanted some of the formalities of a traditional ceremony, and he couldn't wait to see his bride in her wedding gown.

"You okay?" Tate, also formally dressed, asked.

Shane stuck a finger into his collar, hoping for room so he could breathe more easily. "I'm fine. I just want her beside me already." He wanted to make Talia his wife. Have her take his name. Move into the house they'd bought.

Start a family?

They'd begun talking about it.

Suddenly music began and he sucked in a shallow breath.

This was it.

Tate put a hand on his shoulder. "Breathe, man."

He did just that, then turned. Other than Tate, they didn't have a bridal party, just her brother as his best man and Jonah walking her down the aisle.

Jonah, who'd stepped up in the last year to get his wife back. His house had been riddled with bullet holes, so he used the renovation time to move back to civilization and court his ex—who was only too happy to enjoy him acting like a normal human being. He'd shaved his beard, cut his hair, and agreed to some therapy and meds for his paranoia, although he insisted after Talia's situation he really did have good reason to be careful.

The curtains that blocked Shane's view of the door shifted, and Talia stepped forward on Jonah's arm. At the sight of her, Shane's breath caught in his throat.

Talia stood in a fitted white dress, lace on top, what looked like satin below that clung to every dip and curve of her perfect body. And as she moved, a long train followed her down the aisle. He'd never seen a more breathtaking sight.

She joined him, placing her hand in his, a radiant smile on her face. And around her neck was the locket he'd bought her not long after she'd come to see him at McKay-Taggart. Not that it could replace the one she'd been forced to throw away, but he hoped, with the small picture of her mother he'd placed inside courtesy of Tate, that she'd find some measure of peace.

She'd cried when she'd unwrapped it, when she opened it and saw the treasured contents, and again when he hooked it around her neck. She hadn't taken it off since.

"You're gorgeous," he mouthed to her.

He wished he could say he remembered every word spoken by the minister, but he couldn't take his gaze or focus off the vision in front of him. She was radiant, her cheeks flushed, her eyes shining with happiness.

He was fully aware when it was time to say I do.

"I now pronounce you husband and wife. You may kiss the bride," the minister said.

Now that he could do, he thought, and sealed his lips over hers, treating her to a wedding kiss neither one of them would ever forget. After they broke apart, he gazed into her eyes for too brief a moment. Then they were being congratulated by their select guests.

But Shane wanted a minute alone with his wife. He pulled her aside, to a corner of the room, keeping her hand in his. "Hello, Mrs. Landon."

She grinned. "Hello, Mr. Landon. I'm glad we have a minute. I wanted to talk to you this morning, but it's bad luck for you to see me before the wedding."

He kissed her cheek. "I'm here now…and forever."

"Well, that's a good thing," she said, biting down on her bottom lip.

"Because remember that conversation we had about having a family *someday soon?*"

"Yes?"

She drew a deep breath. "Well, that day is now." She smoothed her hand over her flat stomach, but her meaning couldn't be more clear.

"You're pregnant."

"Mmm hmm."

"We're having a baby."

She nodded. "We are."

He let out a loud whoop of excitement, then picked her up and swung her around, his excitement palpable.

"I'm glad it's good news," she said with a grin.

"Hell, yes. It's not every day a man gets married and finds out he's going to be a father all in one day." He couldn't be more thrilled.

This woman was his to love, cherish, and protect. Forever.

Sign up for the 1001 Dark Nights Newsletter
and be entered to win a Tiffany Lock necklace.

There's a contest every quarter!

Go to www.1001DarkNights.com for more information.

As a bonus, all subscribers will receive a free copy of
Discovery Bundle Three
Featuring stories by
Sidney Bristol, Darcy Burke, T. Gephart
Stacey Kennedy, Adriana Locke
JB Salsbury, and Erika Wilde

Discover the Lexi Blake Crossover Collection
Available now!

Close Cover by Lexi Blake

Remy Guidry doesn't do relationships. He tried the marriage thing once, back in Louisiana, and learned the hard way that all he really needs in life is a cold beer, some good friends, and the occasional hookup. His job as a bodyguard with McKay-Taggart gives him purpose and lovely perks, like access to Sanctum. The last thing he needs in his life is a woman with stars in her eyes and babies in her future.

Lisa Daley's life is finally going in the right direction. She has finally graduated from college after years of putting herself through school. She's got a new job at an accounting firm and she's finished her Sanctum training. Finally on her own and having fun, her life seems pretty perfect. Except she's lonely and the one man she wants won't give her a second look.

There is one other little glitch. Apparently, her new firm is really a front for the mob and now they want her dead. Assassins can really ruin a fun girls' night out. Suddenly strapped to the very same six-foot-five-inch hunk of a bodyguard who makes her heart pound, Lisa can't decide if this situation is a blessing or a curse.

As the mob closes in, Remy takes his tempting new charge back to the safest place he knows—his home in the bayou. Surrounded by his past, he can't help wondering if Lisa is his future. To answer that question, he just has to keep her alive.

* * * *

Her Guardian Angel by Larissa Ione

After a difficult childhood and a turbulent stint in the military, Declan Burke finally got his act together. Now he's a battle-hardened professional bodyguard who takes his job at McKay-Taggart seriously and his playtime – and his play*mates* – just as seriously. One thing he never does, however, is mix business with pleasure. But when the mysterious, gorgeous Suzanne D'Angelo needs his protection from a stalker, his desire for her burns out of control, tempting him to break all the rules…even as he's drawn into a dark, dangerous world he didn't know existed.

Suzanne is an earthbound angel on her critical first mission: protecting Declan from an emerging supernatural threat at all costs. To keep him close, she hires him as her bodyguard. It doesn't take long for her to realize that she's in over her head, defenseless against this devastatingly sexy human who makes her crave his forbidden touch.

Together they'll have to draw on every ounce of their collective training to resist each other as the enemy closes in, but soon it becomes apparent that nothing could have prepared them for the menace to their lives…or their hearts.

* * * *

Justify Me by J. Kenner

McKay-Taggart operative Riley Blade has no intention of returning to Los Angeles after his brief stint as a consultant on mega-star Lyle Tarpin's latest action flick. Not even for Natasha Black, Tarpin's sexy personal assistant who'd gotten under his skin. Why would he, when Tasha made it absolutely clear that—attraction or not—she wasn't interested in a fling, much less a relationship.

But when Riley learns that someone is stalking her, he races to her side. Determined to not only protect her, but to convince her that—no matter what has hurt her in the past—he's not only going to fight for her, he's going to win her heart. Forever.

* * * *

Say You Won't Let Go by Corinne Michaels

I've had two goals my entire life:
1. Make it big in country music.
2. Get the hell out of Bell Buckle.

I was doing it. I was on my way, until Cooper Townsend landed backstage at my show in Dallas.

This gorgeous, rugged, man of few words was one cowboy I couldn't afford to let distract me. But with his slow smile and rough hands, I just couldn't keep away.

Now, there are outside forces conspiring against us. Maybe we should've known better? Maybe not. Even with the protection from Wade Rycroft, bodyguard for McKay-Taggart, I still don't feel safe. I won't let him get hurt because of me. All I know is that I want to hold on, but know the right thing to do is to let go...

* * * *

His to Protect by Carly Phillips

Talia Shaw has spent her adult life working as a scientist for a big pharmaceutical company. She's focused on saving lives, not living life. When her lab is broken into and it's clear someone is after the top secret formula she's working on, she turns to the one man she can trust. The same irresistible man she turned away years earlier because she was too young and naive to believe a sexy guy like Shane Landon could want *her*.

Shane Landon's bodyguard work for McKay-Taggart is the one thing that brings him satisfaction in his life. Relationships come in second to the job. Always. Then little brainiac Talia Shaw shows up in his backyard, frightened and on the run, and his world is turned upside down. And not just because she's found him naked in his outdoor shower, either.

With Talia's life in danger, Shane has to get her out of town and to her eccentric, hermit mentor who has the final piece of the formula she's been working on, while keeping her safe from the men who are after her. Guarding Talia's body certainly isn't any hardship, but he never expects to fall hard and fast for his best friend's little sister and the only woman who's ever really gotten under his skin.

* * * *

Rescuing Sadie by Susan Stoker

Sadie Jennings was used to being protected. As the niece of Sean Taggart, and the receptionist at McKay-Taggart Group, she was constantly surrounded by Alpha men more than capable, and willing, to lay down their life for her. But when she learns about a friend in trouble, she doesn't hesitate to leave town without a word to her uncle to help. After several harrowing weeks, her friend is now safe, but the repercussions of her rash act linger on.

Chase Jackson, no stranger to dangerous situations as a captain in the US Army, has volunteered himself as Sadie's bodyguard. He fell head over heels for the beautiful woman the first time he laid eyes on her. With a Delta Force team at his back, he reassures the Taggart's that Sadie will be safe. But when her past catches up with her, Chase has to use everything he's learned over his career to keep his promise...and to keep Sadie alive long enough to officially make her his.

About Carly Phillips

Carly Phillips is the N.Y. Times and USA Today Bestselling Author of over 50 sexy contemporary romance novels, including the Indie published, Dare to Love Series. She is happily married to her college sweetheart, the mother of two nearly adult daughters and three crazy dogs. Carly loves social media and is always around to interact with her readers. You can find out more about Carly at www.carlyphillips.com.

Fearless
Rosewood Bay Series Book 1
By Carly Phillips
Now Available

Fall in love with the Wards...

Mechanic and garage owner, Kane Harmon is used to the wealthy beautiful women visiting his beach town. He doesn't get involved because he knows most females would merely be slumming for the summer.

Except Halley Ward isn't just passing through. She lives a solitary life in a bungalow on the beach. A woman tormented by her past, distant from her wealthy family, different from Kane's usual fare of town girls who know his M.O.- Don't expect more than he's willing to give.

Kane rescues Halley and her broken down car from the side of the road and instantly he's hooked. She says she's not interested in him. He knows she lies. And he makes it his mission to bring her back to life, to return her emotionally to her family. To show her the colors around her were as vibrant as the ones she puts on her canvas.

Until past meets present and threatens all the progress they've made. Then it's Halley's turn to step up and stand up for the relationship and life she's finally coming to believe she deserves.

A Standalone Novel

* * * *

Recognition slammed into him, raw and real. "Halley Ward," he muttered. "Well, I'll be damned." The girl he knew not at all but had protected from bullying back in high school stood before him, all grown up.

"Hi, Kane," she said softly, shading her eyes from the sun with her hands. Eyes he knew were a light blue.

She'd been quiet and withdrawn back then, head almost always hidden inside a hooded sweatshirt, only her two long braids hanging out from her protective armor. But he knew her story.

Everyone did.

This town thrived on gossip, and the Wards provided much of it over the years. In Halley's case, everyone knew she'd been rescued from foster care at thirteen by her aunt but never seemed to adjust to life back home with her wealthy family. She didn't reach out to other girls or make friends at school or in town. Or maybe they didn't welcome her. He hadn't been sure.

He'd only known that, at the time, he had recently lost his mom and pulled back from the world, so he recognized that same sense of sadness and loss in Halley and had stepped in when the kids gave her a rough time because of her past. They'd never talked or bonded, but he knew she appreciated his efforts. Could tell by the lingering, sad but grateful looks she passed him in the hall that his actions meant something to her.

Despite living in the same town, he hadn't seen her in years. That damned gossip indicated she was more reclusive and damned more solitary than he was. She didn't hang out at the Blue Wall, the main bar in Rosewood, on Friday or Saturday nights, at least not when he'd been there. Had he wondered more about her through the years? Sure. But life went on.

"So. Dead SUV?" he asked, gesturing to her ride.

"Dead SUV," she said, sounding pissed off. "What kind of car just... dies? It's not new but it isn't ancient, either." She braced her hands on her slender hips and frowned at her vehicle.

He shrugged. "Won't know until I get it jacked up and take a look." He met her gaze. "How've you been?" he asked.

"Good." She toyed with a strand of hair.

With the sun streaming down, he took in those brown locks with sun-kissed streaks of blonde closer to the ends that hung just past her shoulders. And he immediately noticed that the face she'd hidden as a kid was all the more striking now.

Seriously.

She was fucking beautiful. And still fragile at least in appearance, her skin like porcelain, her features delicate, with a hint of freckles over the bridge of her nose. And there was still that whisper of sadness that fell over her features, there whether she was aware of it or not.

"You?" she asked. "How are you? Still working at the garage, I see?"

He'd had a job there from the time he was a kid, hanging out from a young age, just as Nicky did now.

Kane nodded. "I own the place." He wasn't sure why he felt compelled to let her know.

"That's good." She ran her hands up and down her arms.

"Let me get your truck on the flatbed and we'll go back to the garage. I'll take a quick look and see if I can tell you what we're dealing with."

"Thanks."

"You're welcome to hang out in the front of the cab while I work," he said.

She smiled. "And thanks again." She spun on her low-heeled sandals, and her floral dress, which clung to her curves, spun out around her thighs.

Flirty. Cute. Sexy as fuck.

He did his thing and soon they were on their way back to the garage. "So what's covered in the back of your truck?" he asked, having seen the sheet for himself.

"Paintings. I paint. My work is in the gallery in town. I was taking a few pieces over when my car died and I didn't want the sun beating down and fading them."

"An artist? Damn. I'll have to stop by the place and see your work." He was impressed with that little bit of knowledge about her.

His hands on the wheel, he glanced over. A blush stained her cheeks. "I'm not sure my work is your style."

"Doesn't mean I don't want to see it anyway. Besides, how would you know what my style is?"

"You're right. I don't," she murmured. She curled her hands around her purse on her lap and he refocused on the road.

"Maybe we could change that." Now where had that suggestion come from?

Her gaze swung to his. Startled. "What are you saying?"

"Go out with me sometime." No, he hadn't planned it, but Halley Ward intrigued him. She always had. And now that they were adults, she fascinated him even more.

"I don't date." That surprised him... but it shouldn't, now that he gave it some thought.

It wasn't like he saw her out and about anyway, and she did like to keep to herself. But not to even date? What was that all about?

"Then call it two old friends catching up," he said, now even more determined to find out.

He glanced over to find her lips twitching in amusement she was obviously trying not to show. She might not *want* to be interested in going out with him... but she was.

"We weren't friends," she reminded him gently.

"Do friends stand up for each other?" he asked.

She nodded. "They do."

"Then I'd consider us friends." He looked at her and winked. "Just think about it," he said as he pulled into the garage lot.

Because he was definitely interested in her. Maybe it was fate that her car broke down and he'd been the one to answer the call, bringing them together again after all these years. They were adults now, and he wanted to get to know what secrets she held behind those blue eyes.

Because he sensed, then and now, that her layers ran deep. And he wanted to peel them back and learn what lay beneath.

On behalf of 1001 Dark Nights,
Liz Berry and M.J. Rose would like to thank ~

Steve Berry
Doug Scofield
Kim Guidroz
Jillian Stein
InkSlinger PR
Dan Slater
Asha Hossain
Chris Graham
Fedora Chen
Kasi Alexander
Jessica Johns
Dylan Stockton
Richard Blake
BookTrib After Dark
and Simon Lipskar